Red Gerberas

Red Gerberas

Short Stories

SITOR SITUMORANG

Translated from Indonesian by
HARRY AVELING

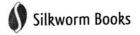 Silkworm Books

ISBN: 978-616-215-150-7

This edition is published in 2018 by
Silkworm Books
430/58 Soi Ratchaphruek, M. 7, T. Mae Hia, A. Mueang Chiang Mai, Thailand 50100
info@silkwormbooks.com
http://www.silkwormbooks.com

Cover: Photo by George Hodan on PublicDomainPictures.net
Back cover: Photo of Sitor Situmorang by Patrick Lumbanraja
Typeset in Adobe Garamond Pro 12 pt. by Silk Type

Printed and bound in Thailand by O. S. Printing House, Bangkok

5 4 3 2 1

CONTENTS

CONTENTS

Life around Lake Toba   113

PREFACE

Best known as a major poet, Sitor Situmorang (1924–2014) also wrote a number of short stories, perhaps twenty-three in all, which were widely admired in Indonesia and abroad. Indonesian critics praised his creation of powerful moods, his ability to present human relationships in a balanced, non-judgmental way, and his use of sparse but highly evocative backgrounds.[1] The Dutch critic A. A. Teeuw considered Sitor's short stores as "belonging to the best which Indonesian literature has produced so far," adding that they "would not be out of place in any modern collection of Western short stories."[2] Fourteen of these stories are contained in this book. The other nine are available in *Oceans of Longing*, also published by Silkworm Books.

1. Nugroho Notosusanto, "Sitor Situmorang," *Siasat,* August 28, 1957, 23.
2. A. A. Teeuw, *Modern Indonesian Literature*, Vol. 1 (Dordrecht: Foris Publications, 1966), 182.

Sitor's roots lay in the traditional world of rural society in North Sumatra. It was here that he was born and spent his early years, surrounded by Batak culture, language, literature, and religious faith. Sitor was an aristocrat and although he left home to go to school at age seven, he returned to Lake Toba at crucial points throughout his long life to fulfill major family and other ritual roles. His grave is there today.

Sitor drew the inspiration for his short stories from a variety of sources. "This Always Happens When It Rains" is a classical ghost story. Two stories are sketches, largely devoted to describing places: "S," about the decaying town of Sibolga on the west coast of the island, and "Life around Lake Toba," focusing on two minor market towns and some of their inhabitants.

As a journalist, poet, and political figure, Sitor traveled a good deal. Most of the stories in this volume were written away from Sumatra. They use other parts of Indonesia (Yogyakarta, Jakarta, and Bali), Europe (Milan), Japan (Tokyo), and Australia (Canberra) as backdrops to the events that take place in the lives of their central characters.

These central characters are all men, except for three stories, which present women talking about men. Invariably these men are mature, strong, confident, open to new experiences, and in control of their own destiny. Usually they are Indonesian men.

The women form erotic others, the objects of male desire. Some are young, barely eighteen. Others are mature and worldly. Often the women are foreign. The meetings are random and the women are changed forever by their intimate experiences with these passing men. Some of the women seek to be "liberated"; paradoxically this is not a condition that is available to men, who have various social and professional obligations to fulfill. They must keep traveling.

In these fourteen stories both the male and the female protagonists are, without exception, spared the existentialist anguish that many critics believe is most characteristic of Sitor's poetry. Anthony Johns, for example, has described Sitor as a poet irrevocably caught "between two worlds," suffering "doubt, loss of faith, and anguish of guilt at abandoning traditional morality."[3] That is certainly not the case here. In understanding the characters' strengths and their weaknesses, and refusing to dwell on their moral choices, the stories aim first and foremost to entertain their readers.

This volume fulfills a promise made to Sitor many years ago to translate his stories into English. My thanks to Barbara Brouwer, his wife, for her patience; to Keith Foulcher and Brian Russell Roberts for encouraging me in this task; to Trasvin Jittidechrak for her belief in the importance of Sitor's stories; and to Joel Akins for his careful editing work.

Harry Aveling

3.   A. H. Johns, "A Poet Between Two Worlds: The Work of Sitor Situmorang," *Westerly*, November 1966, 86.

Sitor in 1957, while in the United States studying film at UCLA.

Sitor and his wife Barbara on the occasion of their traditional Batak
wedding in 1979 at Harian Boho, North Sumatra.

Sitor at the 2010 Ubud Writers and Readers Festival in Bali, where he was honored with the Saraswati Lifetime Achievement Award. Photo by Barbara Brouwer.

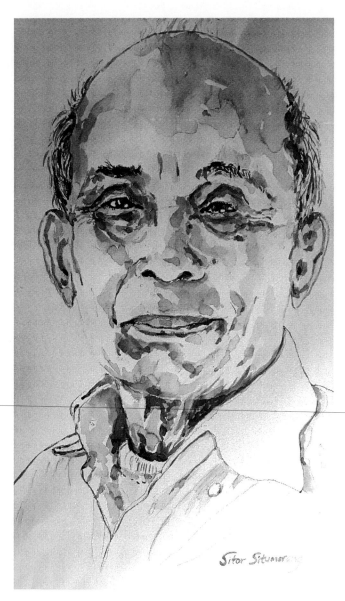

Drawing of Sitor by Erland Sibuea,
based on a photograph from 2012.

GERBERAS

It was a clear morning. The air was like glass. Things moved, nothing made a sound. The mountain wind and the pine fragrance entered our flesh. Our bodies felt as if they were becoming air and floating. We sat on the hotel terrace. Shadows. Tables, chairs, feet (hers), glasses (we were drinking coffee), all floated in the air. The hotel terrace, the courtyard, the pine trees, the mountains, we ourselves, the painting behind a glass. From time to time the lava on Mount Merapi shone in the waves of morning sunlight. This was no painting. Only the steam from the coffee and the smoke from my cigarette reminded us that we were alive. The plains of Yogyakarta spread out below us, to the south and the east. There were people in the city. Millions. Marlioboro, the main street. No sound.

"I was born in Jakarta," she said.

Her eyes shone behind the steaming coffee.

"When?" But I didn't ask.

"I can only drink very hot coffee. I'm used to it."

I did not hear what she said but I understood her. The meaning of what she was saying. And the question in her eyes.

"I lived in Surabaya until I was eight." There seemed to be a question within what she was saying.

"Let's climb this mountain," she said.

"Fine," I replied. With my eyes. But she understood and we rose. We climbed the hill. She led. It was an easy ascent.

I was panting when we reached the top. She was breathing normally and sat on a cement monument. Cross-legged facing Merapi, which soared into the sky. She said nothing and became a monument herself. No one talks to a monument. She pressed her fingertips against my hand on her thigh. I could feel her eyes. They turned from the distance and perched on my forehead. I spoke.

"My eyes. Me." But there were no words. Her eyes swung away again and she was lifted into the air. I looked at her back. She seemed vulnerable.

"It's beautiful!" She sighed.

"I'd like to cross the Alps again," she said in an English that was heavily marked with a German accent.

"People look so small. I wonder who we are." She was not hoping for an answer.

"I've seen the Taj Mahal and now Merapi." Merapi was silent. The blue sky moved away. I lifted into the air and flew beside it.

"That is Mount Lawu over there," she said.

"How do you know?"

"I know it. I know it."

"Look at the lake."

"What is your name?" Those were her words. But she did not expect an answer.

"Look at Yogya. Look at the sea to the south." She, she spoke.

Voices rustled in my head. Not one, not two, but hundreds, thousands. Loudly. My head spun and I leaned against the monument with my head in her lap. Suddenly she embraced my head. With her hands and her eyes.

"I'm lonely. Lonely."

I replied by kissing her. Her lips were cold, as if she had a thin piece of glass in front of them. I kissed her hair, touched her warm and sweaty body. Our eyes and lips were still separated by that piece of glass.

"I was raised in Vienna," she said.

"Have you ever danced to the rhythm of the Donau River? Yes, you must go to Naples, you, we, should go to Naples."

"You can only love once," she said. "The first time."

"What about me?" No one asked that question.

I was silent. She was silent. She released my head. I stood in front of her, facing the monument.

"Do you know," she said, "when my fiancé went to Okinawa, I thought he would never return. So I left Frisco and went back to

Austria. And I came to Indonesia, to Mount Merapi, and I met you, you, you." Her voice was happy, as if she really loved me.

I did not reply.

After that we did not meet for a year. Or was it two?

When we parted I went to her room (I forget where we were. Malang? Yogya? Jakarta?). She said at the time (I said nothing), "Now I really know what it feels like to be in love."

I knew that the words did not have much to do with me. But I reached out my hands. She took my hands and spat into my palms. Then she folded them and said, "Good luck! We'll meet again."

"Where?" I thought to myself. I really wanted to hold her in my arms.

We parted at twilight. I leaned on the foredeck, as the boat headed north, thinking of red gerberas, waving, red as the sunset, as red as her lips.

A year later I returned to the town where I had left her. I don't remember the name of the town. Eventually no town has a name as far as I'm concerned. There have been too many to remember. Too many oceans and harbors. Too many different roads. They look different from one another but are the same when you try to think about them. And I have thought about them. What the towns are like at dawn. Midday. The next day. Sunset. The next twilight. Night and the next night. All the same. Like red gerberas. Red. Red like spurting blood. Crashing into the eyes like an east bound train. Sparkling in a whisky glass. In a river at sunset. Red. Gerberas. Red. Her.

"How is your family?" she suddenly asked me. I was startled.

"Family?" It was the first word I had said.

"What is life?" We were sitting on the terrace to the second floor of a Chinese restaurant. She looked down at the people pushing and shoving as they made their way in and out of the movie theater. I reached for my whisky and drank it.

"Are you happy now?" she asked. And she playfully swept her blond hair back from her face. Her bracelets jangled like the bangles of an Andalusian dancer. Gold bracelets, as thin as threads of cotton, I estimated that she was wearing fifteen altogether.

"Are you happy?" she repeated, leaning back and half closing her eyes.

I looked at her breasts as they pushed against her dress.

Her green eyes sliced through the night. Suddenly she stood up and said, "Let's go to the beach."

I nodded.

When we reached the beach she immediately took off her clothes and stood naked facing the sea, with her arms outstretched as if she wanted to embrace the night.

"Are you happy?"

She did not turn around. I sat on the trunk of a fallen coconut palm. Because I did not reply, she continued: "I'm your wife. I've been waiting for this night."

I stood up and embraced her. Her body felt as soft as a bird's feather. I could have picked her up with two fingers.

She did not turn around but continued to face the ocean. Her eyes still seemed to penetrate mine, boring through my head, and out the back of my skull to the mountains in the middle of the island.

Suddenly I heard thunder in the distance. We turned around. Day was becoming red. We looked. Dawn reddened. Red like gerberas. Gerberas.

When I wanted to speak, she had gone.

Only an empty chair beside mine. Two full glasses of coffee on the table. I stood up and walked to the edge of the terrace and looked at the plains of Yogyakarta. To the south.

One morning I received a letter from her at my hotel in Bandung. Or was it in Surabaya?

There was no mention of who the sender was on the outside of the envelope. But I recognized the writing. It was from her. I was surprised when I read what she had written.

> Because you cannot speak
> I feel like a beggar
> Thank you!
> You can only love
> Once
> The first time.

"Where is she?"

Day after day I walked through the whole city, thinking that every blond-haired woman I saw was the woman from Mount Merapi. But when I came closer, it was obvious that they were someone else. There were no eyes like her eyes—pure glass, but full of feeling and spirit. Her lips were red, like gerberas.

One day I received another letter.

I have met your wife.

You don't deserve a woman like her.

Since then I have never wanted to stay in a hotel. I stayed with friends. But the letters still followed me. Finally I tried to escape her by shifting quickly from one town to another. But her letters were always waiting for me at the hotel or my friend's house. Letters, letters, letters. Her letters pursued me. Sometimes they pleaded with me. They talked about loving once. Sometimes they accused me. I am unfaithful. To her. To my wife.

One day a thought suddenly came: if I stood still, stopped wandering, stayed in the one place, perhaps her letters wouldn't follow me.

I stayed in a house in a small lane, far from the main road and the noise of the city. I didn't go anywhere during the day. I only went out at night. Like a mouse afraid of a cat.

I went out one night. The need to earn money for my daily expenses oppressed me. I walked along the dark lane. In the dark I saw women walking around or joking and bargaining with men. I thought, "If I was a gigolo, I could be like them." I kept walking. Feeling lonely, I greeted a woman standing in the dark at the edge of the road. Another frightened mouse. She was waiting. I was waiting too. Who for? Perhaps for this meeting.

We walked. I told her my story. I told her that I had no money. She suddenly grabbed my hand. When I drew my hand away it held two five rupiah notes.

"What is that for?" I asked but she had vanished into the darkness.

"Perhaps we'll meet again, darling." The voice was harsh and floated in the air like dried leaves rustling in the wind.

I thought I recognized the voice. I ran after her. But couldn't find anyone.

I called a trishaw.

"To the dance hall, the dance hall." The trishaw driver understood.

Two rupiahs for admission. One for the dance card. I danced until late with a well-built girl. When we took our leave, she said, "I'm sure we'll meet again."

"Are you sure?" I replied. But then I added, "Yes, of course, I'll come again. For you. For her. For all of you."

"All of us?" she asked in surprise.

"Yes, all of you. Everyone!" I sipped my whisky. Her eyes reached out, groping through a moonless night. But I didn't care. I left.

In the east, dawn was turning red. Red like the gerberas. Gerberas. Were there still flowers on the mountain slopes?

Tomorrow I would fly west.

AKBAR

A red flower protruded from the barrel of the rifle on the back of the truck.

Akbar watched as the truck quickly passed him. He felt that he understood what an artist might see there.

Nothing had happened around him. The same leaves he had seen twenty years ago were still here. The buggy driver was the same man. He had no one to love.

Once he thought he understood what it all meant. A few particular experiences strengthened that conviction, though he had always been disappointed. When he saw dry leaves fall in the drought, he decided that there was no point in writing a letter to the person who had forgotten him and possibly still loved him.

His success lay in his willingness to postpone things. To perfect the dreams that were part of his loneliness. To stop growth, the blood circulating too quickly. A play of lights from a crystal that had no need to live in the open air. The blood of the drought. His desires had removed all boundaries and made his captivity more bearable. The sterility of his mind was perfect.

Akbar liked the long, straight road. There were seats under a shady tree. He listened carefully to the speakers. But he didn't want to take truth from the hands of other people.

Akbar, Akbar dreamed. He let the sun burn his hair. Blacken his heart. Colder than charcoal. His body floated on the blue reflected in the canal, gazing at the sun. And he knew that people were painting the tram: a yellowish red or a reddish yellow?

His guts tore at him like glass. He knew that one day the hungry would have power. But not over the girl he had raped. Dreaming of seeds spreading in the lap of the dull water. Millions of them.

He remembered the day Elis had used her hair to smile at him, he didn't believe it, the funny way she had spied on him from across the river. It was a hot day in an old town. Elis dreamed inside a dream and knew everything. She was aware of the germs playing on the canal and in the air. She didn't understand her sterility. Elis kept her love for her father. He was dead now but she wanted to make him live within herself. She longed to be pregnant. She wanted to give birth so that she could feel the shape of the object. The object that would ruin the walls of her valley. The tunnel into herself.

That morning she had traveled a long way on the train and become lost in some unknown place. She looked at a shadow wearing black sunglasses. She watched her own movements in a daze. "You are black. Do you think snow is beautiful?"

Akbar had come from a distant country. Far from her country. And the people around her were only interested in the open packet of American cigarettes she held in her hand. She wanted to go to Italy. But she slept in a railway carriage. Now she was heading north. Then she arrived. Arrived as she always did. Because she heard a girl's voice inviting her on the telephone. Then, a long time afterwards: "I remember your voice. The color of your clothing. The way you never spoke. No one dared smile near you."

"I have been looking for you. Just to know what I would never find. So adieu, until we meet again. Maybe I'm too old to understand your irritation."

Then the girl had a child. But she had never rejected young love and was always ready to become old before her time.

But Elis still dreamed, dreamed, dreamed. Her dreams were evaluated differently by other dreams. Serious, or just selling snake oil.

When he was very young, Akbar was often taunted with being a foundling. Horrified, he used to cling to her mother's skirts. After that he never had a mother. The mother he loved had let go of him once she gave birth to him, and was busy spraying the rocky barren earth and dealing with her own hunger, each dry season. But Akbar still believed that he did have a mother. He looked for her in every woman he met. But each woman was forbidden to him by social conventions: the love of a mother, a sister, a lover, a jealous rage. All of these were forms of love. But there was no peace without the admission that what he wanted and what society wanted were unrelated. Thereafter, he could have either flesh or reason. Or neither.

Would Akbar ever get there? Today he was selling poems, which had no worth except as a marker of the recurrence of death.

There was life outside. So much that death was no longer a reality.

The soldier with the red flower in his rifle returned to ask directions.

"That was only an excuse," Akbar thought.

The soldier whistled as he walked away.

CHÉRI

"I think I'll become a nun," Chéri said as soon as Mustafa entered the room. They had agreed yesterday to take a trip out of Paris.

Mustafa was not surprised by her decision. For Chéri everything happened quickly, and as Mustafa was a university student, he believed that problems in human relationships could always be solved.

They were like husband and wife, but the question of marriage had never been broached. Mustafa was nearing the end of his studies and was waiting for the time when they would have to part. He would return to his own country in the Pacific Ocean and assume an important position in the government. Chéri would stay in Paris and look after her old mother. She would meet new friends. And one day in the future . . . Mustafa didn't want to think about that, because he truly loved Chéri, and, at the most, could only imagine being married to someone like Chéri, and only like Chéri.

Could he talk to another woman the way he did with Chéri, who knew him so well that she didn't need to flatter him all the time? Mustafa was very susceptible to flattery. He knew that. He was intelligent but he wasn't confident about this world or the next. He felt a perpetual emptiness that he himself could not fill, no matter how hard he tried. Chéri provided a continual mirror, no matter how slight, which separated him from that void.

Chéri represented the city of millions that validated Mustafa's emptiness, Paris with its aging buildings, its pseudo-intellectual talk about art, and the pleasure of its changing seasons. With Chéri, gossip and the pleasure of the seasons were less tempestuous. Because of Chéri, Mustafa knew that he could live his life even though he had no particular purpose.

These thoughts ran through his mind as he watched Chéri comb her hair, apply her lipstick, and blacken her eyebrows. Mustafa could feel Chéri looking at him in the mirror across her bare shoulder to where he sat, resting on the arms of the divan. He was tired after climbing the four flights to Cheri's flat.

Chéri turned around, took a blouse from a hanger and emptied the pockets. Now she was facing him, dressed only in a bra and her panties. She changed into a fashionable batik bikini in front of him.

Mustafa looked at her beauty. He felt old, although in fact he was only twenty-five and she was twenty-two. He could feel the desire within himself. Chéri seemed not to realize how beautiful she was, like a wild animal. She loved to be caressed, but today Mustafa could only look at her, as if he wanted to preserve the memory, open his senses to every fragrance and sound of the new season, explain his need, and in that way preserve every tiny memory forever.

Mustafa did not say anything after Chéri finished dressing. He stood up and embraced her and, as if nothing had happened, they left the house, after Chéri said goodbye to her old mother in the next room.

They took the bus out of town toward Neuilly, where the Seine curled around the edge of the city and continued to the sea, passing the large park Bois de Boulogne.

The day was hot and the bus was crowded, as it usually was in summer, especially on Sundays.

Chéri had said yesterday that she didn't want to swim, just sunbathe on the riverbank, beside the Bois de Boulogne. The swimming pools were always crowded on days like today.

When they arrived and started searching for a place to settle, there were already a lot of people. Those who were not here yet had already left their darkened houses in Paris. They were coming to fulfill their promise that they would have a picnic with other members of their family, who lived in other parts of Paris, at least once this year. Show off their children, who were one year older, expose them to the fresh air, dip in the fairly clean waters of the

Seine, and run around among the trees, sleep after lunch, alongside the open spaces where the children played ball, and the rustling bushes where couples were kissing and cuddling.

From one year to the next, thought Mustafa, and he looked at Chéri who was lying on her clothes in her bikini. Sleeping, Or pretending to be asleep. He watched as an airplane approached.

Today an old man was expected to jump out of a plane at two thousand meters, wearing a parachute, and, hopefully, land on the Seine.

Across the river, to the west, he could see the Neuilly hills and the villas belonging to rich Parisian millionaires and millionaires from all around the world baking in the sun.

His thoughts and movements unfolded slowly, like the River Seine, the shouts of the children and the teenagers. From one year to the next, thought Mustafa, and this time he was horrified by the boredom of it all.

Chéri was still silent. Perhaps she really was asleep. What would happen to her? Who would look after her in summer when Mustafa had gone? Perhaps that person was already in the world, already in Paris, maybe with another woman, not knowing that he would see and enjoy what Mustafa enjoyed at this time.

Mustafa looked at Chéri's face. Her breasts and belly rose and fell like ripples in a river. He could feel Chéri's blood beating. His blood rushed to his head and he heard a hissing in his ears. Then it subsided. He embraced Chéri. She woke up and smiled at him.

Mustafa wanted to speak but he couldn't. Finally he said, "Chéri, do you want to be my wife? And come back with me?"

Chéri looked at him mischievously and finally said in a sad voice, "We're married already, aren't we? But it won't last forever. One day you'll go. Let me stay in Paris. I would be afraid to leave Paris."

Mustafa said nothing.

Chéri continued, "I don't know your world. I know you and that's enough for me. I only want to know the things that I need. I hope you do too. Everything else is boring."

"So none of this will remain in the future?"

"Stop your nonsense," she said. "All you need to know is that one day I'll be as fat as that woman there."

Chéri pointed at a group of people who were packing to go home.

A fat old woman was busy organizing some children as they dressed. Her grandchildren, perhaps.

"And if you're still as beautiful as this?" he asked.

"Pray that we meet," she replied, "and pray that I still like you as much as I do now."

The fat old woman slapped one of the children and the child began to cry.

Mustafa stood up and went to a tap near a horse trough to have a drink. The trough was left over from the previous century, and the tap was now used by people who liked water better than ice cream.

As he caught the water in his cupped hand, Mustafa realized that he would never know Chéri because she never hid anything.

She assumed he knew that she had cancer. If he didn't, cancer wasn't important and there was no need to tell him about it. Mustafa learned about Chéri's cancer from her mother.

When he returned to where Chéri was lying, Mustafa said, "You're sick, Chéri, very sick. Don't you need me?"

Chéri looked at Mustafa as if to say, "You want me to feel sorry for myself, don't you."

"Not because of that," she said. "I don't need anyone because I'm sick. I need someone because I'm alive and glad to be so. I won't be alive for long. No one lives forever."

People began shouting and pointing up into the sky. A person wearing a parachute was falling toward the ground. The old man whose picture was in the newspaper yesterday.

"He is afraid of dying," Chéri said, pointing to the old man as he swung backward and forward like a sack of rice.

Mustafa looked at the childish expression on Chéri's face.

S

This time I want to tell you about a town which has grown to the point where it has no purpose and is therefore always sad. Its sorrow has infiltrated my heart, just as it has affected the inhabitants, of whom there are not as many as before. It has grown to have no purpose and now it awaits the slow decay of its warehouses. Eventually only the fishermen's shacks will remain, as in the beginning. It is close to the water.

The town is named S.[1] It is on a large bay on the west coast of North Sumatra and faces the Indian Ocean. Everyone knows that not many ships sail along the west coast these days; they prefer to use the east coast and the Straits of Malacca.

The harbor is deserted, except for one cargo ship a month. The town is deserted. It is gloomy, just as the inhabitants are gloomy

---

1. Sibolga. (All footnotes in these stories are provided by the translator.)

while they wait for nothing. From time to time there is the roar of a Chinese trading vessel, going back and forth between the harbor and the Nias Islands. Taking tinned foods and returning with pork for the Chinese inhabitants of S. But the children have no interest in the comings and goings of boats. The buses to the mountains, the high plains of the Batak region, are more interesting. They go to the east coast, to Medan on the busy Straits of Malacca. And from there, people's thoughts fly to Java, riding on the boats to Jakarta. Sometimes they travel even more quickly, following the flight paths of airplanes.

All the thoughts of the inhabitants of S, except for those of the sailors, are directed across the Barisan Ranges to Medan, or even Jakarta, either because the children go to school there or because family have migrated to those places.

But things weren't always like this. S was once the main destination of people from the mountains. As somewhere to sell their incense or educate their children. Or attend to some matter at the court. S was once the capital city of the inland province.

The incense trade had its ups and downs, and they weighed heavily on S. As did the rubber trade. Sometimes people were well off, when rubber was in demand. Mad days when people washed their hands in beer while dining at the food stalls.

Mountain gum and coastal rubber were what grew S fifty years ago. And if a lot was sold, a lot could be bought. Foreign goods were imported from overseas. People in the region were particularly fond of silk clothing.

If there were a lot of goods, then one needed a lot of warehouses. The biggest warehouses were close to the harbor and held incense, rubber, silk clothing, and foreign imports. Related to the warehouses were the offices used to organize the trade: Gijtzel & Schumacher, Geowehry Henneman, Lim Hong Lap, and similar Dutch and Chinese names. There were new shops. A city with straight roads criss-crossing each other in a profusion of intersections. More buses. And at that time picture theaters to amuse the inhabitants.

There wasn't a lot of space, so the buildings were usually several stories high. The mountains and the jungle came down to the shore.

S spread out into the valleys that faced the sea and the beautiful bay. People came down from the mountains in buses to follow the winding roads and enjoy themselves at the beach.

Part of the beauty of the large bay came from the many small islands that were covered with coconut trees. The broad beaches of white sand stretched far out to the sea. The water was crystal clear. When the price of rubber was high, people enjoyed themselves at the beach.

You can imagine them, singing happily to the accompaniment of a ukulele. At that time every young man knew how to accompany himself on the ukulele or the guitar.

Possibly because of these factors, the young men didn't like to leave the region to find their fortunes elsewhere. Because they didn't leave, they also had no access to higher education. There was only one trade school and a few primary schools.

Some people said that it was common for those living in swampy areas to become lazy. Their blood was continually sucked by malaria mosquitoes, one generation after another. I don't know whether that was true or not. But everyone was pale, just as I was.

People with golden-brown skin tended to become pale, like a papaya that had been picked too early. Those with black skin became pale too. But it made them appear to be more refined. They moved at a slower pace. Refined but weak.

Not everyone. The Chinese residents, who made up half the population, never contracted malaria, because they used mosquito nets and slept inside brick buildings. They were healthy perhaps because they ate good food on a regular basis as well. The other half of the population, the Indonesian half, were a mixture of various ethnic groups who lived along the coast and into the mountains. A mixture of Acehnese, Nias, Minangkabau, and Batak ethnic communities.

But the real distinction was between the pious coastal Muslims, who had lived here for centuries, and the mountain-dwelling Batak, who were mainly Christians. The two groups influenced each other and created a new type of society. Those mountain folk who had been away to find their fortunes did not produce children who wanted to leave to find even greater fortunes, which is not what their ancestors had expected to happen when they left the mountains.

A characteristic of the local inhabitants that didn't last long was their willingness to work as hard as the Chinese. A few did, but they did it in a way that fit in with their local customs. They were religious and had their own churches. They lived together in groups at the far side of town, away from the sea, along the roads leading to the mountains, and along the rivers that divided the valleys.

But as far as foreigners were concerned, the most obvious local characteristic was their tendency to drink palm wine and eat pork at the various food stalls, while playing chess and singing together, church hymns that were sacred but rendered joyful by the palm wine they drank. Every afternoon the upper regions of S were full of life and, of course, drunk men. Their favorite song was a tune used to accompany a funeral procession to a cemetery. You can imagine the atmosphere in the late afternoon when everyone had finished working, while the sun was setting and casting its golden rays over the tops of the coconut trees and then the mountains.

The songs sounded sadder once prosperity had passed, when the inland turned toward the eastern coast. And more mountain people took their incense to Medan.

Then the warehouses were empty; so were the Chinese shops with their empty glass cabinets. No one came to the hotels and only the owners lived there, staring at the empty rooms that they could see in the large mirrors along the walls. The heavy white marble tables were useless. And the sound of billiard balls rolling across green felt surfaces vanished and the tables were covered over with cloths instead.

Many other common sounds vanished, and as you walked past the abandoned shops you felt that you were in a large, empty cave. It was very desolate; the only noise you heard was the echoing chatter of sparrows and the sound of the waves crashing on the beach.

In the late afternoon, fishermen fixed their sails and moved out toward the setting sun, singing sad songs, sadder than the hymns that were sung in the palm wine stores in the upper parts of the city. The fishermen's songs advised patience, the wisdom gained from generation after generation of suffering.

The two types of sorrow mixed together in a town that was growing increasingly useless—sad like a bride whose heart and hopes were very high but had then been abandoned before they could be fulfilled.

Many of the inhabitants left, people who were not from this region, especially the employees of the large trading firms and the government officials who were no longer required. The respect previously given to a regional capital was snatched away. The interior regions no longer needed the city and no longer admired it.

The Chinese traders spontaneously left. Many of the warehouses were empty.

One of the two picture theaters closed. It became a refuge for spiders, full of stale air, like the disused warehouses, where men and dogs secretly urinated. A nest for spiders and kites.

Before long, the local inhabitants who remain will only mix with one another in the silence, a combination of the echoing rhythm of the waves as they pound against the beach and the mountain winds that propel the fishermen's boats to the middle of the ocean as they sail toward the golden setting sun in the late afternoon.

And when that day arrives, the palm wine shops in the upper part of town will suddenly fall silent forever.

MIDDAY MAIDEN

For as long as Corrie could remember, or perhaps I should say for as long as she could recall, because she was always trying to recall things, including what she was presently experiencing, and might experience in the future, she had never been outside the big yard.

When she sat like this, looking through the window toward the yard, even when she was asleep, she always knew that she, her life, was inseparable from this environment and the particular mood it contained.

For as long as she could recall, her father's car repair workshop was as much a part of nature as were the bushes and the long grass that grew along the bottom of the wall around the yard, separating her from the world outside.

She had never felt any difference between the decaying, rusting cars scattered around the yard and the plants. No one cared for the iron carcasses or for the bushes and the grass; there never seemed to be any distinction between them, or with the various-colored cars that were being repaired. Nor with the mechanics on and under the cars, dressed in their oil-stained clothes

She knew that her father was one of the men in the garage, but she could never tell him from the others and had never felt the need to do so.

She never heard the sound of panel beating, of welding machines or engines roaring, or the clunking of the printing machines that were also present in the yard. It was a big piece of land and it was her world, ignored by the city around her. The sprawling city did not know about the vast enclosed block of land, just as most peoples' bodies don't know about their insides, their guts and the more obscure hollow parts of their bellies.

Corrie was not conscious of her body; she had never been aware of what she was like. She had never felt lonely here in her corner or been disturbed by the noise of life outside the yard. Her heart beat in as mechanical a rhythm as the passing of the days and nights, even at midnight when night was darkest. The day began with the clunking of the printing machines, interspersed with the rhythmical pounding of her memory.

But sometimes the printing machines stopped, and at those moments the harsh sound of hammers beating on iron thumped against her heart. That was when her father came to drink coffee on the stone terrace under the shade of the leafy trees. Because a certain young man usually followed her father. He was well built, with powerful hands and warm chocolate skin that shone because of the mixture of sweat and oil, especially on those parts of his body where the veins protruded. He was handsome, and knew it, as he set out the bowls, having subdued the clunking of the printing machines beneath his blood, and set the loud hammering roaring in Corrie's heart.

When she left afterward, Corrie could hear her father and the young man talking about problems that had arisen in the workshop. In her heart Corrie was convinced that the time would come when that certain thing would happen. Something disastrous.

Corrie thought that she had never seen the young man's eyes but was sure that they were hard and piercing, as warm as his voice.

So the young man, the new mechanic, simply became a normal part of the landscape inside the whole yard. He was twenty-one; she was seventeen.

She had thought about that thing from the first day when she drank coffee with her father around midday and he hadn't bothered to introduce the young man to Corrie, in his usual way.

Surprisingly, the arrival of the young mechanic reminded Corrie of her mother who lived somewhere outside the yard, in the metropolis of Jakarta. The young mechanic had come, bringing that world into the yard. And he was part of the world where her mother lived. A world that her father seemed not to want to know about, except for the rich men's cars that had been involved in accidents and needed to be repaired. The workshop was filled with cars that were being repaired, and sometimes the presence of the handsome lords who owned these vehicles, and even their ladies on occasion, but seldom with the men who drove them. At least the lords looked handsome to Corrie. Her father treated the lords as though he were a doctor and they were parents of sick children. They needed him. And he was a cold-hearted car "doctor."

"Father never says anything about my mother," Corrie thought one day soon after the young mechanic began working at the garage. Corrie looked at the photograph of her mother in the silver frame by the window. Who was she? Was she really so sweet and beautiful? Had she lived like Corrie? Riding around in a car perhaps?

Corrie thought about those things after the arrival of the young mechanic.

"I need a young assistant," her father had announced one night. I'm old and I need someone who can take over from me. None of my present mechanics have the ability to run the business.

"I need a rest."

But Corrie knew that her father could not and would not sit around like some superannuated figure, even if he was old and worn down by life's hardships.

Corrie suspected what he wanted. And why he had chosen a Eurasian like themselves.

"You must be lonely here." She had never known any other life but this. When she thought about it, she realized that she had been about four years old when her mother ran away with a lord who owned a car. It hadn't seemed like a catastrophe at the time. In fact, there was no sense of connection with her mother. On the contrary. Her major feeling was that her mother did not belong in the workshop where the family lived.

Her mother's bedroom was small but somehow different. She hadn't realized how different the room was from its setting until the young mechanic came.

After he arrived she often studied her naked body in the large mirror, and remembered how her mother used to lie naked on the bed. Like her mother—especially when the weather was very hot—Corrie ran her hand over her body until the blood pounded in her heart in time with the repeated hiss of the welding machine.

Some time that thing would happen. "It has already happened," she thought. Her blood suddenly began to flow quickly, then stopped. The door creaked and the young mechanic stood there. She could see his large powerful hands. They were stroking her flesh. Corrie lay back naked in her mother's bed and the young mechanic's sharp eyes stabbed her like the eyes of a wild animal.

"It has happened," she suddenly thought.

His rough warm hands groped over every part of her body, as if seeking to release her long pent-up desires.

"It has happened," Corrie thought with horror. She could no longer hear the hammers pounding on metal.

The thing that had happened was heading towards a mixture of destruction and pleasure.

And the young mechanic released everything that had been imprisoned in her body.

After he left the room, she continued to lie back with her hand outside the sheet, across her body. Her legs were intertwined, as if trying to stop something flowing away and vanishing.

Corrie felt a moist drop and turned her head to one side, so that she could see herself and especially her breasts in the long mirror.

Her happiness was mixed with horror, the sound of the hammers, and the hiss of the distant welding machine.

Her happiness floated on the sound of the printing machines. Her blood slowed, like a river that had finished hurrying through the rapids and was now crossing a flat plain, peacefully heading toward the ocean

Corrie stood up, her heart beating in tune with each step she took and each movement she made, with every sound she heard outside.

As she looked through the window, she felt her blood flow in time with the world around her and she understood her mother now, alive in the room and the yard, in the flow of her blood around the whole city where her mother was.

Her father, who had once been Corrie's only world, was beginning to fade, shoved to a corner of her mind, now she knew that he was busy organizing something, perhaps buying spare parts in a shop, like thousands of other people who lived and worked so that they could survive in the metropolis.

Corrie took her mother's picture and kissed it. Somewhere outside she knew that the young mechanic was busy with the welding machine.

THIS ALWAYS HAPPENS WHEN IT RAINS

I was half asleep and reading the newspaper when I wrote this story. Impossible? I'm sure you've heard about an author who wrote a short story while he was talking to someone else. My story is even more amazing. I wasn't talking to anyone.

It happened in a restaurant in Menteng, Jakarta, near the railway line. Night had fallen. If I tell you that there was a heavy downpour, you will know what it was like. I'll stop for a moment.

"Stay awake!" someone or other said. There were only two people in the restaurant. Night had fallen a long time ago. There wasn't much traffic. I looked at the two other customers. They both looked away when they met my eyes.

Light from the electric poles made the rain on the tracks sparkle. The last train blew its whistle. Then the light shone on a path, revealing the figure of a woman walking there. The woman seemed to be frightened. I was concerned that she might stumble into a ditch, but once the train had passed she reappeared out of the darkness and headed for the restaurant.

She stood dripping wet outside the restaurant. For a moment she was uncertain—should she come in or not? Her white blouse was made from thin material.

"Come in," I said encouragingly. "Wait here until the rain stops." She looked at me and started to walk toward my table. From the corner of my eye, I could see the two other customers watching the girl. The new customer was still a young woman. But her gaze was powerful and seemed to reach out from another, very old, world. Surprised, I shivered. I passed her a handkerchief so that she could wipe her hands and face. Then I lent her my comb. She accepted all these gestures as if I was an old friend, or a lover.

"Thank you," she said. Her voice was sharp but somehow distant. The expression in her eyes was like that too. I was briefly surprised; then I realized that I hadn't offered her anything to drink.

She calmly sipped at her cordial.

"Why are you so sad?" I asked, uncertain how to begin.

"I'm lost. I tried to take a short cut to Old Gondangdia in the dark."

"This late at night? And in the rain?"

"It was flooding."

"Flooding? There hasn't been that much rain. Gondangdia is close by and there isn't any flooding here."

"No, there's nothing here."

"She's a bit crazy," I thought to myself. "What a pity. She's quite an attractive young woman."

"Are you waiting for the rain to stop, sir?"

"Yes, I am."

"Could you please escort me to my house?" Her voice was as sad as the falling rain.

"I'll take you there."

I could smell the fragrance of tuber roses.

"What are you drinking?" asked the owner of the restaurant. I suddenly realized that I hadn't drunk anything for a while.

"I'll have another beer."

"Another beer," the owner shouted to his assistant. Half an hour later the rain began to ease. The two other guests had left and the owner was packing up, preparing to close the restaurant.

We left.

There were no trishaws around. When we reached the corner of Jambu Street, she said, "There used to be a cemetery here." Then she walked over to a dark place by the side of the road. "I need to go," she said.

I walked a few meters away and did not turn around. "It is hard for a woman when she needs to pee on a main road," I thought. But no one would see her in this heavy rain . . .

When I heard chains drop I instinctively turned around.

"Have you finished?" I called out. There was nothing there. I waited for a moment. Nothing moved. I could hear a car a long way away. There was still no sign of the girl. I didn't know if we were any closer to where she wanted to go. There were no bushes or drains where she could be hiding. No fences. Had she gone into a house? I waited a few minutes longer. Beginning to feel nervous, I shouted, "Hello? Hello?" My voice probably didn't sound very convincing. I was becoming very anxious. I picked up a rock and threw it. Maybe I was the one who was mad. Then I felt angry. "Meow!" A cat, not a woman.

"Damn you, cat!" I walked away.

But as I walked, I felt uncertain and turned around again. And I saw something white beneath a tree. Her rolled up blouse. I took the blouse and opened it, trying to see if it could tell me something. A sweet smell began to pour from the garment. I threw the blouse away and started to run. I was frightened.

As I ran, I remembered that she had told me she lived in Halimun Road, number 12. I remembered that clearly. The address was rather a long way from where I lived. But I felt that I wouldn't feel comfortable until I knew what was happening. There were several houses made of bricks and woven thatch panels. The numbers of the houses were written on the walls in curly tar figures. I knocked on a door. After a moment I saw an old woman through a window, coming to open the door. She peered through the window then undid the latch. The woman invited me in. I sat down as she spoke.

"A white blouse? That would be her. My child, Mariana. She died when she was still a small child, five years old. If she was still alive she would be eighteen today . . . the twenty-seventh of November."

"Mariana?"

"Yes, my name is Mariana," the girl had told me.

"Why are you so sad?"

"It's a nice name, I like it," I said. "Eighteen is a beautiful age."

"Why are you so sad?" she asked me.

The train rails still shone.

"I'm shutting the restaurant now," the owner said in slightly annoyed manner. The newspaper fell from my hands. The girl was obviously not in front of me. It was starting to rain again.

First Love

As an Italian girl from a traditional family, I am fortunate to have had plenty of opportunities and the freedom to pursue them, including the chance to visit various countries in the Far East, Indonesia in particular.

I went there for the first time a year ago, when I was seventeen. My father (who was still alive at that time) and mother were very concerned about giving me the permission I needed to apply for the visa to travel while I was still so young. Finally my older brother calmed them down and they let me travel such a long way.

What helped them finally decide, so my parents told me after I came back, was a young Indonesian man who quite by chance appeared when the trip was still being discussed. That night some kinsfolk arrived from Mantua, where my parents were born. They had been deliberately been invited to Milan by my father, to join in the campaign to encourage me to change my mind. About dinnertime at my parents' house, because I was the only one of their children who had not yet left home, the kinsfolk, who were actually my brother and sister, arrived with a foreigner, whom they introduced as their friend. He was an Indonesian.

Before then we had met a few Asians, business friends of my brother. They came from India, Thailand, Indonesia, and elsewhere. I liked meeting my brother's friends because I could act as an interpreter and secretary when they came to Milan.

I finally went to Indonesia as my brother's secretary. Besides English, I had studied basic Indonesian from some books and practiced with the Indonesians who visited Milan, and I was in contact with the Indonesian trade attaché in Milan almost every day.

To that point in time, all the foreigners I knew were business people. So the young Indonesian man whom my brother invited was something special.

"This is Mr. —," my brother said. "He is a journalist, an Indonesian. And he's visiting Milan. I met him at the trade attaché's office. I thought he should meet a real Italian family tonight."

The young man was rather reserved. I don't know what impression we made on him that night. We often have that sort of meal. My sister is married and lives in Mantua, and my parents miss their grandchildren, so it is always lively when they visit. My father pretended to be concerned about my travels because he never likes disagreeing with my mother. My mother swung between approval and disapproval, as was obvious from the way she expressed her fears and her doubts. I saw how her gaze frequently shifted between the young Indonesian man and myself.

"Look how handsome he is!" my brother said. "You don't have to worry about sending Silvana to such a beautiful country. Does he look like a cannibal?"

Mother gave a hollow laugh and seemed somewhat embarrassed in front of the young Indonesian.

"Sign up, sign up," my brother said in a joking tone. "If you put your signature there, Dad will do it too." My sister took some ink and an old fashioned pen from our father's desk.

I was sorry for my mother as she added her signature to the form my brother produced from his pocket and set out on the table for her attention. Briefly she looked at the young man and said, "Please look after my child. Please look after her."

The young man nodded and glanced at me. I was only seventeen.

My blood pounded when our eyes met. He was very handsome, I thought, perhaps because he looked so exotic as far as I was concerned, and perhaps because he looked so serious as well.

That was how my trip to Indonesia in connection with my brother's expanding business came about. My brother took me to Bali after he had finished his meetings. I cannot tell you what a lovely time I had there. The music, dancing, everything, it was like a dream. Because we have poverty in Italy and our culture is very old as well, nothing I saw and experienced in Indonesia seemed strange. Especially because we were in constant contact with the young man. As far as I was concerned, he was a mixture of the newest and the most ancient that his country had to offer.

We went everywhere with him. And we often sent postcards with him to my mother. Once he wrote beneath my letter, "Silvana hasn't been eaten by cannibals. Not yet, anyway."

When I arrived back in Milan (shortly before my father died), Mother told me how she and Dad laughed at the young man's comments.

He has passed on now. I can't leave Mum like that in order to go on long trips.

So I was pleased to hear from my brother that the young Indonesian was planning to visit Milan again, on his way to attend a journalism conference to Geneva.

The young man wrote to me, asking me to buy three tickets to the La Scala Opera, meet him at the station, help him find a hotel for such and such dates, and such like.

I wondered if he'd written to my mother or my brother about the visit.

For some reason, I didn't ask my mother's permission to go to the station. I just went. If mother had received a letter she would have told me, wouldn't she? I thought. But why hadn't I told my mother or my brother about the letter I received?

I went straight to the station from my office.

My heart was beating rapidly as I entered the railway station. I felt as if I was being dishonest. Everyone who passed surely knew of my feelings and why I had come to the station.

I had to wait another five minutes before the train arrived from Rome. I was nervous. My hands trembled. A porter knocked me with his trolley. I apologized for his mistake.

In the distance I heard the train whistle and the roar of the locomotive. Another minute and the train from Rome would be here.

Suddenly I went, or I was impelled to go, and hid behind a pillar. I could not even see the train from Rome pull into the platform. The cigarette vendor watched in amazement; he thought I was playing a game. I immediately decided to buy a packet of cigarettes and a box of matches. The vendor looked at me suspiciously.

Quickly I put the matches and the cigarettes into my pocket. Then I left the station. I had never smoked.

I was startled to see my mother in the crowd around the stairs. Feeling embarrassed but also happy, I caught the tram home. When I arrived home, I saw a piece of paper on the table:

Silvana,

I have gone to the train station to meet the Indonesian gentleman. He is arriving today. Please cook some spaghetti. He will stay with us.

Mother

The Indonesian gentleman, as mother called him, did indeed stay at our house.

I moved to my mother's room, he took over my room.

At dinner mother proudly said, "Silvana cooked the spaghetti tonight."

Later the three of us went to the Opera. Mother was very happy. The Indonesian gentleman sat between us. He didn't say much. When he did speak, it was mainly with my mother. The opera was Verdi's *La Forza del Destino*.

The music was wonderful. I don't know how the Indonesian gentleman felt. I wanted to ask about this and that but when I looked at him in the dark, I couldn't speak. At interval mother asked me to accompany her to the cloakroom. There was something she needed to do urgently.

When we reached the cloakroom, she surprised me by saying, "I'm going home, Silvana. I'm tired. Stay with the gentleman. I can take a taxi by myself. But don't you be late coming home after the show."

She put on her coat and left before I had a chance to comment.

On my way back to the auditorium I met the gentleman in an aisle.

He smiled when he saw me.

"Where is your mother?" he asked.

"She has gone home," I replied. "She was tired and apologizes."

"Would you like a drink?"

"I don't need one. We should go back to our seats. The show is about to resume."

We went and sat down. The music began, the curtains opened slowly as if moved by the rolling pulses of the pathetic music.

"Silvana," the gentleman whispered, "your mother saw you at the train station."

I did not reply. The music filled my soul and carried me away.

That was the first time we were together. Two days ago. And yesterday he continued his journey to Geneva.

Mother ordered me to take him to the station. Just before the train left, I realized that I still had the cigarettes and matches in my purse and gave them to him.

"Were you worried that I wouldn't have enough money to buy my own cigarettes?" he joked.

"No, I was worried that you wouldn't have enough Italian to ask for what you wanted." It was a bold reply and not at all typical of me.

"When will we meet again?" he asked with a laugh as he boarded the train.

"Whenever you want," I said. "I'll cook spaghetti when you come."

"I don't think I'll be able to come back," he said. "Italy is such a long way away."

"Who knows?" I replied, sounding very experienced.

"No, I won't." he said. "Ever."

"Why?" I asked.

The train began to move. He looked at me with a smile on his lips.

"Ask your mother."

I walked alongside the train as it slowly pulled away.

"Ask your mother," he repeated. "I promised her. Arrivederci!" He waved. "Look after her. She needs you. Give your mother my regards."

Was that what they call "first love"? I wonder. Before then I had never thought about love between a man and a woman, certainly not in connection with myself.

But I know now that something in me had changed, even though mother continued to treat me like a child and I looked after her.

Tomorrow I will go to church and pray that my mother will be blessed. I will light a candle for Our Lady, Mary. Tomorrow is my eighteenth birthday. May mother have a strong faith that will comfort her in her loneliness. I am leaving.

PRINCE

A good time to visit people there is just before six o'clock, when the sun is setting. A house with a big yard, high above the main road, the wide road that goes around to the east of Yogyakarta. On the other side of the road, ripening green rice fields stretch to the horizon and blur in the distance. There is probably a volcano far away.

Prince, my host, was seated in a rattan chair, waiting with his wife. I called him "Prince" at his own request.

Prince stood and held out his hand to invite me in. The gateway was covered with a flowering shrub. His wife wore one of its blossoms in her hair.

Twilight added a special touch to the scene. To their reception of me. The house and the yard. The well kept lawn and the usual shrubs, almost at random: coconut palms, limes, mangoes, at spaces allowing for plenty of room for a flower garden, except that there weren't any flowers.

"We have a vegetable garden over there," Prince said. "Itinerants work it for us."

The house and yard had been an inheritance.

In one corner, near the gate into the yard, was a place to pray, a meditation area facing northwest. Or perhaps towards Mecca. Or the peak of Mount Merapi.

I hadn't expected Prince to be wearing a sarong but it suited him.

We talked about the nobility.

"I can only remember a little," I said. "Anything more than that disturbs me. The world is a very different place now."

Prince defended himself against both things. Against the nobility and against the modern world, which is too given to a sense of relativity.

"I can understand the attraction of the mystical," I said. "But I only like the mystical when it has a human cause."

I relaxed into the mood of our discussion, like a king enjoying his own fantasies.

Prince smiled.

I said, "If a human being hasn't done it, there is nothing mystical about it at all."

We ate together, served by his only son.

A prince among princes, says the teller of the tale. As night approached someone played the *gender* xylophone in the rotunda.

The room where we sat and ate was full of fine Chinese furniture. The main colors were black, gold, and red. It felt full despite the sparseness of the furniture, the openness of the room reflecting the openness of the world outside.

His wife had left us.

Just two men together.

Japanese Proverbs

Every effort to explain what I meant had failed. It was past midnight. The owner of the restaurant and the waitresses were packing up, ready to close for the night. They all looked at me at different times and indicated, "I'm sorry but I can't understand you".

When I wanted milk, I drew a picture of a cow and a glass. They brought me a glass of milk.

I wanted to know if the restaurant was open all night, as many restaurants are in Paris and London. The gestures I made and the pictures I drew only confused them. They shook their head and said apologetically, "Gomennasai!" Sorry.

I was confused and didn't know what to do. But I was hungry. I heard the voices of three young women. They laughed and joked as they entered the restaurant. They were dressed in Western-style outfits.

The youngest wore a flared skirt. She looked at me in embarrassment when her skirt caught on a bonsai pine tree growing in a large pot near the door. Perhaps she was upset that a foreigner had seen her. She released her skirt from the tree.

As she passed me, I asked her, "Do you speak English?"

She stopped near my table and replied, "Sukoshi!" A little. Smiling, she held up her fingers to indicate a small amount.

I told her what I wanted to know, holding up a picture of a clock and imitating the movement of the hands on a plate.

"Wakaranai," she said shaking her head, I don't understand. Without my inviting her to do so, she sat facing me, ignoring her friends, who had already occupied another table. They smiled.

I offered to buy a drink for the girl and her friends. Without any hesitation, they accepted my offer. Before long, the four of us were chatting together as if we were old friends—laughing, smiling, and looking at each other.

My intended stay in Tokyo of two weeks turned into four weeks. The small girl in the big flared skirt became my constant guide. Every night, except Sundays, she worked at the Queen Bee Nightclub, near Tokyo Station, welcoming the customers.

On Sundays, the girl and her friends took me to some of the tourist spots around Tokyo. We worked it out together. Hayama beach, the temple city of Kamakura in the South, the Hakone mountains (Japan's "Swiss Alps"). At the end of those four weeks, when I was getting ready to go to the airport, I received a phone call from the small girl in the big skirt, wanting to say goodbye. Kimiko Mizuhara, as she was known, was ringing from a movie theater, where she and her friends were watching Tony Curtis in "Trapeze". Could they come with me to the airport? The conversation ended with the words, "Gomennasai, gomennasai. Sayonara." We'll see you soon.

Three months later I received a letter, written in English. The first sentence said, "Time is flying, like an arrow." She told me about her two friends. They still visited the tiny restaurant regularly after finishing work at the nightclub.

She no longer lived with her friends but had moved close to Ueno Station. If I ever visited Tokyo again, I should look her up. The letter was signed Kimiko Yoshida.

On the outside of the envelope, she had written her old name, Kimiko Mizuhara. I sent a postcard in reply, "Congratulations!" I assumed that she had married and changed her name.

Shortly after that, I received yet another letter from her. It was composed of short notes, translated directly from Japanese and taken from her diary.

7 August. After work at the Queen Bee Dance-hall, the three of us—S, T, and myself, we share the same house and work at the same place—went to eat at the Yamoto restaurant, near Tokyo Station, as usual. A dark-skinned foreign man asked us to have a drink with him. Then he invited me to be his guide while he

was in Tokyo. The three of us took him to the Station. When I asked them, S and T said that I should accept his invitation. I told them that I was a bit nervous. They said I could just go out with him during the day. On Saturday night and Sunday, we could all go out with the foreigner, if he wanted. There would be no danger in that, S and T told me.

10 August. After we watched a baseball game, the foreigner invited us to go to a Noh play. He had already bought four tickets for the afternoon show. None of us had ever seen a Noh performance. The foreigner doesn't understand much Japanese but he seemed very interested in traditional Japanese culture. Apparently he has read a book by Chikmatsu, or at least heard of it. We laughed when we heard him pronounce that name.

12 August. We watched Kabuki today. The foreigner had two complimentary tickets. I don't know who gave them to him. But somehow he always seemed to have the best seats wherever we went, and he never paid for them. It became much clearer when I saw his picture in a film magazine. He was at Toho Studios, with Riki, a famous Sumo wrestler, and Kishi Keiko, my favorite movie star.[1]

1.   In the mid-1950s Sitor visited Tokyo in connection with a film that he was making about the Japanese military occupation of Indonesia. (See J. J. Rizal *Sitor Situmorang: Biografi Pendek 1924-2014,* pages 36–38.)

15 August. We visited Hayama Beach. In the bus he kept saying, "It's just like Indonesia, the houses and the way people live are exactly the same." The foreigner looked at the houses very carefully.

We had a room provided for us at the beach. The foreigner was reluctant to change into his swimsuit in front of us. S and T teased him. I picked up his clothes and put them in the basket with our clothes. We have never felt so happy or liberated as we were on that day. S and T both told me that.

I can't say whether the foreigner was shy or not. But he treated us with such respect that we sometimes felt rather awkward. When we climbed into the bus, for example. Or as we walked towards the beach. He insisted on carrying our heavy bags, which contained our swimsuits, towels, and such like.

He seemed to like the beach. The foreigner looked at everything in amazement. Swimming didn't interest him at all. He came in the water once, after he had blown up the rubber tube I had brought with me. He didn't say much. When S and T started to swim around us, he swam back to the beach and left us. S and T were disappointed. They both liked him.

When we reached the beach, we found him throwing a ball with some Japanese teenagers and a few American soldiers. He gave them some cigarettes and laughed, as if he had forgotten all about us. They drank cans of beer provided by the American soldiers.

On our return to Tokyo, he took the three of us to eat in a Chinese restaurant. I was amused when S and T said that he must be filthy rich.

He never offered me money or anything else. I felt free when I was with him. And happy.

17 August. He was absent today. He told us that he had to go to his country's embassy to celebrate their Independence Day. I was lonely and stayed home to wash the pile of clothes that had accumulated since I had become his guide. S and T mocked me, saying that I was thinking about him too much. I excused myself when they invited me to go to an afternoon matinee, saying I didn't want to go anywhere.

I decided not to work that night and meet him at his hotel instead. When I telephoned him, he answered and we agreed to meet in front of Tokyo Station.

The foreigner invited me to see folk dancing in the parks. There are folk dancing competitions all over Tokyo during summer, one neighborhood against another.

I almost told him that I had won a beauty contest in our district, a few summers ago. That night he asked me if I considered myself a geisha. I told him that I didn't know. Was I a taxi-girl? "Probably." He asked me this and that about my education and how much I earned at the nightclub.

I understood what he was saying but I didn't want to talk about myself in English. He proposed a simple solution. I should show him photographs of myself and my family, beginning from my childhood.

18 August. I took my photo albums to his hotel. The foreigner looked at the photographs one by one. He said very little, except to ask occasionally, "That's you, isn't it?"

I think he found out most of what he wanted to know by looking at the albums. They covered my life and that of my family quite thoroughly, from when I was a little girl right up to when I won the beauty contest a few years ago.

19 August. I wanted to explain about my life to the foreigner. While we moved from one photograph to the next, I listened to my own stories as though I was listening to someone else. He was so interested that it was only late in the afternoon he realized he was hungry.

We went to a small restaurant near a river. The foreigner liked small, dingy restaurants, the sort that working-class men go to. He shared his bottles of beer with the men there.

20 August. It was almost one o'clock at night. I was taking the foreigner back to his hotel when someone (I found out later he

had been sent by my "master") grabbed me on the stairs of the hotel and dragged me into a waiting taxi.

I was startled and sad but I couldn't fight the man. The taxi took me to where my master was waiting with a "guest" I'd never seen before.

Angrily my master said, "He only wants you!"

All night I thought about how the foreigner might misunderstand me. I was sad that I couldn't explain anything to him.

There was only one hope! I had left a bag of shopping at the hotel, containing clothing and cooking utensils, when we walked away from the taxi.

The bag was a guarantee that we might meet again. I was pleased.

22 August. I telephoned him early this morning. He was still asleep. I was afraid that he might have gone out. Surprisingly, he was very friendly; he hoped that I might come over in the middle of the day, so that we could have lunch together. I didn't disappoint him!

That morning, he had several things to organize: his airplane tickets, telegrams, and such like. He was getting ready to travel on to other lands.

23 August. We ate lunch together then went and watched a movie.

The foreigner didn't say much. He asked me if I wanted him to buy anything. I told him that there was no need to buy me anything.

After the film we went to drink coffee at a café with a jukebox. The jukebox had a lot of French and Italian discs. I don't like that sort of music very much. The foreigner apparently did. We spent a long time at the café. The name of the restaurant was very strange: Jurien Soreru.[2] The foreigner said that was the name of the main character in a famous French novel.

I prefer Calypso music. (And classical Japanese music.)

The foreigner said, "Can we visit your parents?"

I replied, "They wouldn't understand. They never do." He gave me a sympathetic look, as though we were old friends, very close friends. I felt that we, the foreigner and I, were like brother and sister, abandoned by our parents. In fact, the foreigner would never fully understand my feelings, my customs, my history, the life my family had led, even though he assured me he had learned a lot from the photographs I had shown him in my albums.

I want to be free!

The foreigner said, "You are free! It is we men who are not free!"

---

2.   Julian Sorel is the main character in *The Red and the Black,* by Stendhal, published in 1830.

I told him, "You understand me, sir." I called him sir because he was much older that I am.

The foreigner replied, "I know that many educated young Japanese men are suffering psychologically because they need to find liberated Japanese women and not women who are still slaves to traditional ways of thinking."

I asked him, "Do you like geishas?"

The foreigner said, "As an ideal they are a fine . . . but in reality, liberated men must be accompanied by liberated women."

I didn't understand what he meant.

But I couldn't possibly introduce him to my mother. She already thinks I'm a prostitute.

24 August. It was his last night in Tokyo. He didn't want to go back to his hotel. We watched a movie. He would be gone in the morning. I wanted him to ask me to come to the airport with him. I'd never been there. But I suspected that his Tokyo friends might want to go with him. I would be out of place.

There wasn't much we could talk about, so we went to another movie. Afterwards we had dinner at a restaurant near Ueno Station. It's a district of students and artists. I knew the foreigner would like it more than other places.

He told me how much he admired Japanese art, as he studied the Kanji written on the boxes of matches set out on the table for visitors to the restaurant.

I was very tired. He was too. I suggested that what we wanted to say could wait for the morning.

25 August. He was leaving in the morning. He snored as he slept on the floor of the tiny hotel. I woke him with the sound of my filling the teapot the owner of the hotel had slipped around the door of the room.

It was a wonderful morning. An airplane flew low above our head, its engines roaring as it cleared the rows of houses.

The foreigner said, "I'm leaving on a plane like that one!" He laughed.

I went to find a telephone. S and T said they weren't worried. I certainly wasn't. Time is flying like an arrow!

There was nothing more in the letter. I've transcribed it all. Except for the postscript: "The last sentence is a Japanese proverb."

Four years later, in 1961, I visited Tokyo again. The first chance I had, I tried to find Kimiko's address, hoping she hadn't moved. I wanted to know what had happened to her. Visiting Tokyo without seeing her, without at least trying to find her, seemed like moral neglect.

It was spring and the weather was still cold. Snow had fallen on Tokyo the day before I arrived. Was she a good mother and housewife? That she might have died never crossed my mind. I might meet her by chance. We could bump into each other in the crowded city of many millions of people and not even recognize each other. Every morning the road around the Imperial Palace was jammed with demonstrations by laborers. Could Kimiko possibly be in one of those processions?

A few days later, a hotel official finally found her address. Late at night, after I had returned from watching a film, I read a small piece of hotel notepaper that had been placed on a small table under a reading lamp, near the bed: "Kimiko Yoshida is now Mrs. Kimiko Iwasaki. Address —. Telephone —."

I immediately picked up the telephone to ring her. A stranger, possibly her maid, answered. Then Kimiko herself spoke. "I'm glad you've come," she said, happily and almost innocently.

"I have a child now. A boy."

We promised to meet the next day, at the statue of Hachiko the dog in front of Shibuya Station, near the street where she lived, at precisely one o'clock.

The following day, I waited at the place we had chosen, where people often arrange to meet each other. Shibuya is one of the largest train stations in Tokyo and is always very busy. Promising to meet in front of it means participating in the seasonal rhythms of the common people's life in Tokyo. Everyone from school children to grandparents wants to meet there, even if it is only to enjoy the fragrance of the early morning spring atmosphere. Paper sakura flowers served to spread the sense of disorder to the streets, shops, and surrounding buildings.

Precisely at one o'clock, I saw Kimiko. She smiled. Surrounded by crowds of people, she made her way toward me, holding a two-year old child by the hand.

Kimiko was wearing a green woolen sweater she had knitted herself. Her frock and shoes were old and worn. And when we shook hands, her palms suggested that she was now used to hard work. Her face was reddish, indicating her pleasure in life and her delight in being a mother.

"Shake hands with Uncle," she said. "This is Yoshiko." The cute child immediately reached out his hand to me. Kimiko chose the sort of cheap restaurant we were used to. As we ate, Yoshiko played around the table. His mother fed him mouthfuls of noodles from time to time. The waitress looked at us with undisguised amazement, especially me.

Kimiko explained, "The gentleman is an old friend."

Yoshiko accidently stubbed his foot against Kimiko's chair. Although he cried, he was probably exaggerating his suffering in order to attract his mother's attention. Kimiko let me pick him up. I sat him in my lap and stroked his head. Kimiko said, "His father spoils him."

Yoshiko groped for his mother's breast, like a baby wanting to be suckled. Embarrassed Kimiko looked at me, and said, "He likes to act like a baby when he's hurt."

"I don't mind," I said. Kimiko bowed her head, uncovered a breast and suckled Yoshiko. It didn't take long to console him.

The scene was more beautiful than many a statue or painting. I turned away and looked at the busy road. The season encouraged the people of Tokyo to dream dreams.

After lunch, Kimiko invited me to come and see her house.

"I have a shop," she said. "We sell small goods and spices. My house is made of bamboo. You're welcome to visit us when you come to Tokyo."

"What does Mr. Iwasaki do?" I asked.

"He works at Tokyo Station," she said. "Or he used to. Now he works in the office of a trade union. There is a strike going on and he hasn't been home for the past few days. Yoshiko doesn't see much of him. He comes home after Yoshiko has gone to sleep and leaves again before the boy wakes up."

I sensed that it was pointless to discuss her husband.

"Are you happy?" I asked.

"I work hard during the day," she replied with a smile. "There isn't time to think whether I'm happy or not. I don't go to the movies any more."

"What happened to your two friends? Where are they now?"

"They're both married. One lives in Nagasaki. The other one lives in Osaka."

"So you're the only one who has stayed loyal to Tokyo?" I commented. Kimiko did not reply. She simply smiled.

When we reached her house and the shop, she invited me into a very small room. We sat cross-legged and she offered me a cigarette. The shop attendant was surprised by the sight. We were facing the television. It seemed that the television ran day and night, without ever stopping.

Yoshiko played with one of the cigarette packets scattered around the room.

"I'd like to work in your shop," I said. "And stay in Tokyo."

Laughing, Kimiko replied, "I wish I could travel around the world the way you do."

"You've done more than travel around the world." I said.

"That's true. I travel in my mind with you."

"Is that another Japanese proverb?" I asked.

"I'm sure you know," she said. "Proverbs arise from the way we live. People in this land are the prisoners of their proverbs. My husband is trying to create new proverbs."

There were more people coming to the shop now. Apologizing, Kimiko stood up and went out into the shop to serve a small boy who wanted to buy an ice cream.

I followed Kimiko to the shop. She was selling cigarettes. The shop had run out of the particular brand the customer wanted.

"Please get me a carton from on top of the cupboard," she said, pointing at a stack of boxes on top of a cupboard in a corner. She dragged a chair over for me to stand on.

"You'd make a good shop assistant," she said. "When you get tired of wandering about, you can come and work here."

I stayed in Tokyo for another two weeks, visiting her when I could and working in the shop. Sometimes I took Yoshiko for a walk. I bought him a brown bear. Kimiko thought I was spoiling him. I never met her husband.

When I returned to Indonesia, my image of her husband had grown. He was a hero in a postmodern love story.

Kimiko did not ask if she could come with me to the airport. Holding Yoshiko on her hip as she stood outside her shop, she waved as I drove away in a taxi.

"Sayonara," Yoshiko said softly.

Jatmika and Jatmiko
(A Parable)

Two mousedeer lived in a zoo. Their names were Jatmika and Jatmiko. They were twins, even though they didn't have the same mother and father, because their family history was not dependent on ties of blood, the way human beings are. They were twins because they lived in one place and studied with the same religious teacher. Besides that, they were almost the same in every way.

In the society formed by the animals in the zoo, Jatmika was considered to be a very wise mousedeer, while Jatmiko was considered to be very cunning. But because they were so alike, no one could remember which one was wise and which one was cunning. Their speech was almost the same too, because they liked to borrow each other's phrases and use them in community meetings.

One day the zoo was turned upside down by the arrival of a new inhabitant, a black bear. The creatures were amazed by something very strange about the bear. The black bear had a red jacket, which he liked to display on the fence of his cage in the early morning. The mousedeer could see it very clearly

Jatmika, the clever one, said, the first time he saw the coat hanging on the fence, "What a beautiful sight! It's just like a modern painting."

Jatmiko, the sly one, replied angrily, "What do you mean? Beautiful? The color offends my artistic sensibilities. Especially when a bear wears it. Anyway, why is he wearing a coat when we are not?"

Jatmika: "The choice of color is a private matter, but I think the sight still has artistic merit. On the question of whether he should have a jacket or not, it is my opinion that you and I don't need clothing, our skin and fur are beautiful enough to protect us. They are smooth and are easy to rub clean."

Jatmiko was contentedly rubbing his forehead. "You're right about our skin and fur, but I don't think anyone else should have a coat like that unless they ask our permission first. Doesn't he know that Lion is the king of the zoo, but the director has entrusted the maintenance of law and order to us? The black bear doesn't realize that relationships must be civilized, and that comes from clever creatures like you and me. Lion can roar. The bear can growl. But we mousedeer have to think about what is best for the world."

Jatmika: "Do you think that the bear wears a jacket because he is cold?"

Jatmiko: "It doesn't matter what his reason is. He should ask us first. I'll tell the director, so that he can take action."

Jatmika: "Wouldn't it be better if we spoke with the bear? Perhaps he has a good explanation."

Jatmiko: "Please yourself. You talk to him. I don't want to put myself on the same level as him by talking directly with him."

Jatmika: "All right, I'll call him. Hey brother! Comrade Bear!"

The black bear was standing sunbathing near the fence. He turned toward the mousedeers' enclosure.

Jatmika asked him, "Hey comrade, we want to know, why do you wear a jacket? And a red one at that."

The bear turned and stared at the sky before answering Jatmika. "I'm amazed to hear you ask that."

Jatmiko: "Why are you so amazed? Don't you realize that you're the only creature in the zoo that wears a coat? And a red one at that."

Bear bowed his head and replied: "It is purely a coincidence that the jacket is red. I'm amazed at your question. The fact that I have a coat is a whole other story.

But I'm amazed that you haven't asked me how I came to be here."

STORY OF A LETTER FROM LEGIAN

I t was already late at night when the last flight into Bali landed from Jakarta. I hoped to meet her at Legian, along the beach past Sanur, in a cheap hotel at Kayu Ara, near the location of the Goddess of the Sea shrine, to the north. According to her most recent letter, I could ask for directions from Ronald, a Frenchman of Spanish descent, a mime artist who lived here because he was fascinated by Balinese theater, a pleasant man who was probably a homosexual, who apparently smoked carefully regulated amounts of ganja.

When I arrived at Ronald's shack in the dark, he had clearly moved to another place in Kayu Ara. So I decided, because it was so dark, to look for a cheap hotel in Sanur and go to Kayu Ara in the morning, when I could see where I was going. To my surprise, all the cheap hotels were full, and the better-quality hotels were too expensive. There was no choice but to start walking again, even though I was a bit nervous in the dark, accompanied only by the pounding of the waves, without any human presence. There were not many houses along the seashore between Sanur and Legian, the few that existed were empty because of the rainy season, left in tatters by the strong winds that blew off the ocean.

I did run into two or three people of uncertain social status, none of us spoke to the other, the mood frightened me. I thought of a French girl, a thin woman, who lived alone in a shack among the thick weeds with her small child, the result of her sexual promiscuity. It wasn't clear who the child's father was. People said that the unmarried mother might commit suicide one day. I heard that from Julia, the young German woman from Hamburg whom I was planning to meet. Julia was footloose; she had spent the previous two years in Bali after living in Yogyakarta for a while, where she first studied traditional Indonesian dance and theater. When she was a teenager, she had belonged to a professional theater group in Germany before deciding that she must go to Indonesia, a richly stocked warehouse of ideas that could be applied to modern theater. Balinese theater in particular was famous throughout Europe, having been praised by the most famous of all modern theater theoreticians, Antonin Artaud, who was a prophet in Paris during the 1920s and afterwards widely revered throughout the whole of Europe. He died in a madhouse during the 1930s.

Julia was a typical 1970s intellectual. She found Bali at the same time the hippies did, though she was not really a hippie. She knew what sort of work she wanted to pursue, to be an independent woman, earning only a small salary, derived from her many years of involvement in *wayang* shadow puppet theater, and with the security of having her parents as a back up in Hamburg. Her father was a doctor, a very famous professor of medicine, who often traveled to what he called "the third world" in order to improve instructional standards, as part of various "aid" programs.

She was not a feminist. She shared and worked with men as an equal, without experiencing any discrimination, being an artist just as they were.

However Julia admitted that, having lived in Indonesia for the past two years, she was now suffering a severe psychological crisis. She did not belong in her old world, Europe; she was not yet fully accepted in her new world, Indonesia. She lived in an Indonesian way, the way the poorest artists lived in Yogyakarta and Bali. She had almost married, after living for a year with a young Yogya actor, but at the last moment she decided that she should stay single if she wanted to grow and pursue a career in the theater, hoping she could produce a work that could prove that, through a process of "self-alienation," she could triumph over both East and West. She enjoyed climbing the slopes of live volcanoes in Yogya by herself, and she had climbed Mount Agung in Bali alone as well. When people in sacred sites asked her if she was "pure"—not menstruating—she lied.

In Kayu Ara, Julia lived in a luxurious housing complex that had been abandoned by its sponsors because of their incompetence and lack of promotional skills. She had been told that the complex was a project of Club Med, a tourist organization that arranged holidays for the world's super-rich in which they could sail around in pleasure boats and visit the most exotic parts of the globe.

It didn't surprise me that she lived in such a place, even though I knew she was not financially well endowed. The road to the complex was winding and the night was still dark when I arrived. The complex was close to the beach. There were plenty of the usual recreation areas. The style overall was a mixture of Tahiti and Bali. Small lights glowed in carved stone frames under the coconut trees that were scattered across the front of the courtyard.

A guard took me to the very last bungalow. The others were obviously unoccupied. They were still new but even in the dark I could tell that if they were left unoccupied for even a short time, they would quickly decay. Julia's bungalow was not locked. A hanging kerosene lantern illuminated the room. It was very luxurious, just like a room in an international hotel. It was compact and made good use of wood. Despite my fears, it did not smell musty.

I looked around the room carefully. The guard returned to his post. Suddenly I heard the roar of a bus and the chattering of a group of passengers. Japanese tourists. The bus roared again. Then giggles, from a group of local women. Sex tourism, I thought.

The cover was pulled up neatly on Julia's bed. A cloth lay over the table next to the bed. There were other signs that the room was inhabited. The bathroom was very neat. It smelled of bath soap. Where was Julia?

I had come to work on a script for a dance pantomime. Julia and I had been talking about it for a long time. We wanted to mix ideas and movements from all over the world in order to create a work of nontraditional theater. Two cultures face to face, fighting and loving, coming to know each other, possessed by each other, the anger of the local gods, volcanoes exploding, mutual attraction and sexual conflict, body against body, pushing and shoving, embracing each other, bodies united, but . . .

The Japanese tourists had scattered, each one taking his partner to one of the bungalows. The wind and the booming waves echoed the busy sounds coming from the various rooms.

The guard was certain that Julia had not gone far. It was obvious that she was nearby but it was not certain where. My eyes fell on a thick envelope that had been placed under an earthenware lamp. I took the letter. It was a long letter in Julia's hand. I recognized the writing. When I counted the pages, there were thirteen in all. She had signed the letter and added some erotic sketches. The letter was dated October 16, 1976, two months after we had first met in Yogya at the home of one of my theatrical friends. Since then we had become rather good friends, although I left it up to her to decide where, when, and why we would meet. The meetings were to be spontaneous, with no subsequent obligations. We had met several times over that period and separated without difficulty each time. We sent each other letters as well. She wrote far more than I did. The letters included entries from our diaries and monologues, mixed with practical requests about things we each needed, as we moved between Yogya, Jakarta, and the place where she spent the most time, Bali.

One night the three of us were walking together in Bali: Julia, Ronald, and me. We had been to visit a young Spanish man, the son of a millionaire who lived in Barcelona. The artist made gorgeous coffee table books. He chose the pictures, wrote about them, and published them himself, all at his own expense.

The young man lived in a studio he had erected on land rented from a local farmer. It was a long building, extremely modern, and equipped with a separate kitchen and bathroom at the back. He slept on a thick rubber mattress. The ceiling above the bed was covered with Nepalese mandalas, presumably to help him and his partner when they practiced Tantra. Julia resented his lifestyle, and probably felt jealous of it as well. He had no worries. His father in Barcelona supported him fully. He could pretend to be engaged in creative work.

"Bullshit!" Julia said one time after we left the Spanish photographer's studio. Julia wasn't usually vulgar. In response to the hateful young Spaniard's hypocritical "bourgeoisie manipulations," she tore off her blouse and walked naked beside us on the beach.

Beneath the pale light of the moon, which had just emerged from behind a cloud, she then began walking more quickly, letting the waves splash over her feet and the salt cling to her hair, her ritual for merging with nature and seeking inspiration. She was very aware of her huge breasts, which made her look like a whitey Durga.

I wondered if Julia had left her house and gone out tonight, to walk naked along the beach.

I began to read the letter.

Dear S,

I have just completed an extraordinary journey today. You'll see the wounds I have endured when you next meet me. Ronald and I spent two weeks wandering around the rice fields and temples of East Bali. We began at Sukawati, not much of a start. We stayed in a temple, as the unexpected guests of a high caste family. Their condition is very pitiful, revolting in fact. He spent most of his time picking his nose. The atmosphere around the temple was like a plantation in the southern states of America. It was like something out of a Tennessee Williams play. We were glad to get away. That night we watched odalan; it was the first time that Ronald had witnessed a masked dance performance. We both enjoyed it and talked to the actors after the show.

The next day we met a famous performer while we were walking toward Batuan. He told us that he was dancing in a masked drama that night. In Wetu Bulan. We left our backpacks and walked through the villages and fields to the temple the performer had mentioned. It took us six hours to get there. The walking was easy. We stopped at about ten different food stalls. And we bathed in the river when we reached Banyar Tege in the late afternoon.

Ronald and I wore sarungs. I also wore a shawl and a Balinese style blouse. People were delighted. Somehow it made them friendlier. That night we stayed with a family. The arrangement came about because as we were bathing in the river, we met a member of the family and he invited us to stay with them whenever we wanted. The actors for the evening drama were also staying there. About eight o'clock they began rehearsing the drama. I'm not exactly sure what it was about because they improvised a lot. I'm beginning to be able to sense when the creative spirit plays a part in Balinese dance and drama rituals.

I'll keep this short. Otherwise I'll be tempted to go on forever and give you every possible detail. After Tege, we went to Candi Dasa. We were invited to watch the Calon Arang story in a particular village that night. We walked to Tenganan, a Bali Aga village, while it was still daylight. The center was just like an ancient Roman village. The houses were lined up in a row. It was beautiful because it was so old, but rather gloomy as well.

17 October.

I have lots of free time now to write to you. I'm sitting on the bed with my legs folded up beneath me.

The Calon Arang performance at Tege was very funny. It was presented just to amuse the local population and had no ritual value at all. The performance took place inside a house, on a Western-type stage. As you would expect, I didn't like it at all and I fell asleep. Of course they made me sit in the front row. Before the show Ronald and I had looked for somewhere we could sleep. We found an empty temple in the middle of some scrub. We had both drunk a lot of rice wine and eaten far too much pork. A gentle breeze made it impossible to stay awake. It wasn't easy finding some peace and quiet. But it was very pleasant sleeping in the temple. Just before Rangda appeared, one of the actors invited me to watch from behind the screen. He was someone I knew from Batu Keling. I drank more rice wine while I watched the show from behind the screen. When the show was finished, all the actors lay on the floor, pretending to be dead. Rangda returned to the cemetery. The show was over. We crowded back onto the truck to go home. We were bumped about worse than being on the ocean. Bodies flew into the air each time we drove over a pothole. The wind was very strong. When we reached Candi Dasa, Ronald and I said goodbye to them. And we promised to see them again.

We did nothing for a day.

Now I'll tell you about Bugbug. Ronald, Suprabe and his father, and some others decided to climb a mountain. We left in the afternoon. Neatly dressed, of course. When we began our climb, we were surrounded by hundreds of people, including lots of children, carrying offerings and roast pork. The climb was fairly easy. The view from the top of the hill was unbelievable. The branches of the frangipani bushes were covered with roast pork and baskets of offerings. The crowd was enormous—5,000 people on the top of the hill. Far below us, we could see the ocean, the hills around Mount Agung, the rice fields, and the scarred earth that had been damaged in previous eruptions.

Suprabe's father is an old man. He has no teeth. Ronald treats him as if he were his own father. The old man explained something or other to us. I have never known what his name is. He drinks rice wine all the time and chews betel nut. When Ronald is drunk, he will go anywhere with the old man. After the ceremony was over, our friends left us. We decided to stay the night on the top of the mountain.

I stopped reading. Without realizing it, I had stretched out on the bed. Outside, I could hear the sound of the wind. The wind was far louder than the crashing of the waves. The Japanese men were singing softly. They were drinking sake or the local *brem* and behaving as if they were back home at a geisha house. There was a diary near the kerosene lamp on the round marble table between

Julia's bed and my own. I took it and flicked through the pages, without feeling any guilt for violating her privacy. Many of the pages were full of erotic drawings in india ink, and calligraphic expressions of her own experiences and opinions about sexual relations. The pictures and sentences were realistic but never vulgar. More honest and more direct than Kate Millet's doodles. Millet is an American feminist-painter-filmmaker-novelist-poet who gained international fame for her paintings and photographs on the themes of lesbianism and eroticism. In my opinion, Julia's drawings were extremely masculine. Were they sublimations of her unconscious? Julia was a liberated woman but never cynical or frustrated about masculinity and feminity, unlike the present generation of European feminists who consider masculinity and femininity to be absolute opposites. The door creaked. It was the guard looking in to ask me if I still wanted to wait.

He was obviously still here.

The lamp the guard had used to bring me to the bungalow flickered as the wind from the sea passed across the front veranda. There was a blanket on a bamboo chair, and another table on the other side. Plates and glasses sat on the table, covered by a cloth. I went out to the veranda.

The guard said, "Julia likes to disappear at night. She walks along the beach, bathes in the sea. She's not afraid of anything."

He invited me to sit down and eat, saying that there was enough food for two people. I remained standing, with the letter in my hands. I was indeed hungry and suddenly remembered that I hadn't eaten since I was on the plane. I had spent many hours looking for accommodation, walking along the beach, feeling cold, tired, nervous, and even afraid, walking through the darkness of Bali at night. There were many things to frighten one here, even if one proclaimed a thousand times that one did not believe in ghosts or tempting demons. As I ate, I continued reading Julia's letter, despite the poor light of the two lamps. The guard had taken the lamp from inside to brighten the veranda.

S, I want you to know what happened that night. There were about 5,000 people. They had come from far and wide, bringing their offerings, pieces of roast pork. After ten o'clock, men started becoming possessed, they ran around holding daggers in their hands and carrying boxes and other things on their shoulders. They were gambling, eating, and drinking. It was a Dionysian orgy. I began to understand the meaning of Balinese magic.

Ronald and I looked for somewhere quiet to sleep. The moon was full. It hid behind the clouds, came out, then hid itself again. People were amazed by our preference to rest somewhere quiet. About four o'clock in the morning, I woke. Rain had started to fall. Ronald was not there. Three men stood near me, surprised that I was alone. I told them that I was not alone. My friend had gone to relieve himself. Nothing more than that. After waiting five minutes, Ronald had still not returned and one of the men touched me and asked why I was alone. Wasn't I afraid? I told the man that I was fine, he didn't need to worry about me, and I asked them to go. I was beginning to panic. Rain continued falling. My voice grew louder, Finally Ronald did appear. He had gone to find his shirt, which he had dropped on the way up the hill. Fortunately the rain wasn't too heavy. We climbed up the hill, toward the temple we had found before. There were still a lot of people around, but the situation was much calmer now. To our surprise, the atmosphere was really rather beautiful. We moved away and fell asleep again. When we woke, the sun had risen far into the sky. We were surrounded by twenty to thirty people, who were staring at us in disbelief. I needed to change my clothes. We didn't want to be stared at. But more and more people gathered around us. Their mood was decidedly hostile. However, they slowly began to understand who we were and what we were doing and they went away, leaving us by ourselves.

The walk down was beautiful. Some of the men who had stayed behind to guard Bugbug last night were now taking their turn to climb the hill. Most of the stallholders had folded their stalls and were walking down the hill, with their equipment on their head. We chewed on some mangoes, confident that we could wash the juice from our hands when we reached the bottom of the hill. The "river," as they called it, was actually a canal, dug out in a channel created by a lava flow, reaching from Mount Agung to the sea. We looked for an uninhabited place where we could bathe in the river. As we bathed, we heard the sound of a gamelan. We joined a procession and returned to Bugbug.

Bugbug is a barren and unattractive town. The courtyard to the temple is very wide, big enough for all the pilgrims. We spent the whole day there. In the late afternoon we went back to Candi Dasa but we returned to Bugbug in the evening, accompanied by Pak Prabe. The young people were dressed beautifully and performed some very strange dances. Then some older dancers went into trance as they each played the role of Krishna. The contrast with the earlier performance was striking. The young dancers were like models. The old dancers spoke with the gods.

We stayed with a very kind family. Bugbug was a good place to bathe. It had a public bathing area just like the Romans used to have. The moon was still full.

The next day we returned to Candi Dasa. I wanted to meet Mrs. K. Eventually she arrived from Den Pasar, accompanied by three young Dutch girls and a few Javanese and Balinese women. She made an impressive figure. I waited, hoping to be introduced to her. But she was much too grand to take any notice of us. Ronald scampered off to somewhere or other. Suprabe said that we were invited to have breakfast with the guests and Mrs. K. It was all very formal, in my opinion, just like meeting the queen.

After she had made small talk with the guests, Her Majesty came and sat on her throne. She deigned to ask me what I was doing in Indonesia but hardly looked at me when I told her. I felt I was being examined. I didn't like it. My answer was rather confused.

After we were allowed to leave the table, I plucked up my courage and asked Mrs. K if I could show her some photographs I had taken. She replied immediately. No. I went to find Ronald and we packed our things. I was sad leaving Suprabe and his father, who were friends of Mrs K. Otherwise I was happy to go.

(I could imagine the vast gap between a young Western artist like Julia and the local aristocracy faced with her liberated ways. They probably thought that she was a hippie. Julia described their small talk: the hostess didn't eat pork. That was why she liked being with Jews and Muslims!)

Back to Julia again:

Before Her Majesty arrived, we were all sitting around on woven mats and our beds stuffing ourselves with pork—save me from the privileged classes! While we were leaving, Mrs. K offered us coffee and asked about this and that. She told us that she had been to the theater in Europe. It was wonderful! Then she said Indonesian teenagers could learn a lot from watching performances like that. Next she said that she had heard about me from various people. The German ambassador had mentioned me at some function or another in Den Pasar. Or Jakarta. She wasn't sure. What a hypocrite! I was more than ready to go.

We took a van to Ubud to meet Robby and Debra, two friends who hang out with Mrs. L, a rich American woman who had opened a yoga center, together with her Indonesian husband. The center was full of exotic antiques. I hadn't seen Robby and Debra for a long time. They told me that they had been sick. Robby's foot had been in a plaster cast. They had a baby. Their paintings were getting bigger and bigger. Ubud was too crowded these days. As they hadn't met Ronald before, they also told him all their old stories, gave him advice—be nice to the locals, help people but don't expect any reward for what you do, this is not the place to make money—exactly the same things they told me the first time we met, when I was still an inexperienced newcomer to Bali. It was no wonder that Debra soon drifted away to do something else! I felt as though I still don't know the secret to this place.

The next day we lost ourselves among the rice fields. All day. Finally we reached our friend Johny's shack. He lives in the middle of a sea of green. We slept there.

Then on to Trunyan. A village head we had met in Badung told us that there was to be an important three-day festival in Trunyan. From Penelokan we walked to the lake, then headed for Toya Bungkah, along the inland road, past volcanic wastelands. The black lava on the ground was sharp and hurt our feet. We danced our way across it, much to the amusement of the fishermen on the lake.

I stopped reading for a moment and stared out through the dark toward the beach. I thought I'd seen a shadow. Maybe it was Julia returning from meditating by the edge of the ocean. I was right! Julia emerged from the black night. Her body was wrapped in an old batik sarung cloth, the sort one wore for bathing. She walked with a stick and dragged her left leg. Her hair was uncombed. Her Durga breasts spilled out from the top of her sarung. After calling out "Hello!" she threw herself into a chair and said in German, "Wie geht es!" (How are you?). I looked at her in amazement, unable to say a single word. Then she continued, "I see you've been amusing yourself reading the letter I never sent you. It is so full of mundane things. Anyway, you were coming today so there was no point in sending it. I'm glad you found it."

Finally I managed to say, "Where have you been? It's so late. Visiting someone you know around here?"

The story was very ordinary. She had sprained her ankle walking on the lava from the slopes of Mount Batur. As she had explained in her letter, the road was full of people out to have a good time. Because of her ankle, she had spent the last few days resting on her bed. Finally she became bored. After finishing her dinner at eight, she went to the beach to wait for me—"ambush" me—by the mouth of a small river, which was the only way to get to her beautiful bungalow. She was sure that I couldn't cross without her knowing about it and without me seeing her waiting there.

Obviously I did escape her trap and somehow I failed to see her as well.

It was well after midnight when she returned. The peaceful mood her story had created was disturbed by the sounds of the Japanese tourists and their companions preparing to leave for their hotel in Sanur. They were sex tourists and had never properly stayed at the bungalows. Julia was the only real guest at the complex.

She could explain that. The "manager" had offered her accommodation when she was having trouble finding somewhere better to live than a cheap hotel or a shack like Ronald's. She didn't have much money at the time. Julia accepted, recognizing the possible risks that would be incurred when he demanded to be "rewarded for his services." Then she further explained why she had decided to wait for me on the beach. Ronald had vanished the past few days. He had run out of marijuana. The so-called manager started coming around in the afternoons. His intentions were perfectly clear. His words slid this way and that as he conveyed his hopes, and he offered the possibility of even more services if Julia would only be a little friendlier. Julia decided to stall him: Someday, maybe. With a sprained ankle, and possibly a foul-smelling infection under the bandage, she couldn't possibly think of making love!

That was the situation. The night was dark and the two of us sat inside the bungalow, with the remains of the food and the two

kerosene lanterns, while the guard slept outside on the veranda.
The wind blew more loudly. The waves pounded against the beach.

In the morning I looked for a cheap hotel in a village near
Kayu Aya where Ronald was supposed to be staying, except that
we had not seen him. After finding one, I slept all morning, then
dozed for the rest of the day.

Late that afternoon I woke up with a headache. I rented a
motorcycle so that I could move around. First I went to Ronald's
shack. A villager explained that he hadn't been around the past few
days. Then I went to Julia's bungalow. She wasn't there. I continued
driving towards Legian, to Kuta, following the paths through the
rice fields. The paths were several hundred meters away from the
coast and couldn't be seen behind the trees and the thick foliage.
The continual sound of passing traffic made their existence obvious.

When I reached Kuta I went into a restaurant crowded with
young tourists. I knew I wouldn't find Ronald or Julia there. Then
I went back to my lodgings to wait for what might happen next.
Perhaps Julia or Ronald would try to find me. But I hadn't heard
anything by nightfall. The guard told me that Julia hadn't been back
to the bungalow since my unexpected arrival. The bungalow was
tidy and everything was in its proper place, despite Julia's refusal
to lock the door when she was away.

In the evening, I returned to Kuta to read the newspapers. I
was half inclined to go back to Jakarta. There didn't seem any
way of carrying out the project that had really brought me here,

which was to complete a script for Julia's dance presentation. The intention was to create "a new form of culture" based on all the conflicts that existed throughout the whole world. My eyes were suddenly arrested by a small headline in a local newspaper: "Tourist couple found dead on Legian Beach."

Was it suicide? Or were the waves too big for them? Their bodies had been found by local villagers. The newspapers gave only the first initials of their names: J and R. I sat stunned in my chair. Was it possible? Certainly it seemed possible. Julia and Ronald dead. They could have committed suicide together. They could have drowned while recklessly swimming in the ocean, oblivious to the dangers of the fierce waves. It was impossible to tell. Perhaps they were high on drugs.

Julia's letter was still in my pocket. I took it out and began reading from where I had stopped before, just as Julia had suddenly emerged from the dark. The next part of the letter said,

During our travels we danced for the fishermen on the lake, despite our sore feet. Everywhere we went we met young men and women who always seemed ready to celebrate the various festivals, even in the midst of fields covered with black lava. They were beating gongs and using tin cans as xylophones. For some reason, I felt for the first time that our troupe should be prepared to go anywhere and play under any conditions. In Toya Bungkah we stayed with a traditional healer, ate at their foodstalls, bathed at the springs near the beach and beneath their restaurants, ate fish fresh from the lake, and took the ferry to Trunyan. Ronald has been to Trunyan three times. He tells me that the people there do not encourage visitors, and everything is very expensive. Visitors have to pay to enter the temple, to take photographs, and so on. Tourists need to be careful or they will have their pockets picked and their belongings stolen. But when I was there I didn't experience anything like that. I suspect that if people come for only twenty minutes, the Bali Aga might not be very well disposed toward them.

(A European girl sat on the other side of my table, together with her boyfriend, a young Balinese man. From their conversation, I gathered that all tourists were keen to trap a partner, whether they were traveling with a group or by themselves, just as they were always ready to dance on the sharp black lava from Mount Batur that was extra hot during the drought season. I couldn't believe that Julia and Ronald were dead, killed while seeking thrills in the peaceful or the ferocious ocean. I imagined them laid out in the hospital mortuary, waiting for their country's diplomatic representatives to be told what had happened to them. I didn't know where Ronald came from in France. Hamburg is a major international port and would not grieve the loss of one of its honorable citizens. The whole of Bali was an ashram, not just Mrs. K's center. She might have been a grand lady and a real snob, but she meant well and was kindly disposed toward "the Balinese people," who were her own people, even if they lived somewhere else. Julia had seen that for herself. But now it was too late to change things. Julia was dead.)

I continued to enjoy reading Julia's letter, far from any thoughts of death. I felt as if she were with me, her heart beating beside me. What was real and what was illusory—death, life itself, the world? She had explored the successes and the miseries of Balinese culture.

"They have only twenty minutes to exploit the tourists," she had written.

It is such a sad relationship between the vendors and the visitors. They have such different values. Ronald and I had come with empty purses. We walked back to Toya Bungkah because we didn't have the four thousand rupiah required to take the ferry. We stayed at an almost-empty cheap hotel at the luxurious modern arts center. Perched at the foot of Mount Batur we waited to explore a sacred site that was almost perfect in its isolation. Attended a seminar on "The future of culture: The culture of the future." Dreamed beautiful dreams, inspired by the dream of Bali itself. (When we don't have any money, we even stay away from cheap hotels. There is no law against staying away from cheap hotels.) A friend took us to the main bus station in this island of gods (or demons) when we left three days later.

Trunyan was amazing. The people were good looking, despite the hardness of their faces. As usual, we wore local clothes, and that brought us closer to them. They gestured thumbs-up as we passed. We witnessed the initiation of teenage boys. A coming of age ritual, an extremely old ritual, which only happened every five or ten years, so we were told. The ceremony began about eleven o'clock. Sixteen boys were to be initiated. They came out one by one, wrapped in dry banana tree leaves, carrying staves, and wearing old wooden masks (just like the masks worn in Africa or New Guinea.) The frightened onlookers ran out of the temple courtyard when the dreadful creatures suddenly began to chase them. The leaves they wore were considered to be sacred. If someone took a leaf from them and ate it, that person would never grow old. The onlookers did their best to take a leaf. The young men chased them for hours on end. Ronald was hit with a staff. So was I, across my back. The only people who weren't attacked were old people carrying babies and mothers calmly making offerings. These women passed undisturbed through the chaos.

Some people offered cigarettes in exchange for a leaf. Ronald was so caught up in the mood of what was happening that he offered his knife, his shirt, and even a sarung. We were continually given cakes. After several hours, the boys began to faint. Their costumes made them very hot. People fanned the boys to revive them. Some boys went into trance and had to be restrained.

About four o'clock they ran to attack other parts of the village. About six o'clock they took off the banana leaves and ran and jumped into the river, stark naked except for their masks, which they retained.

I stood up and walked from the terrace of the restaurant toward the beach. The tide was rising and the waves were covered with froth. There was hardly anyone on the beach.

I felt calm. It was not certain that the foreign girl I read about in the newspaper really was Julia. Perhaps the people who had been asked to identify them had only guessed that they were Julia and Ronald.

For two years Julia and Ronald had lived in Bali, exploring every beach and mountain they had come across. They had been involved in virtually every ceremony and celebration, whether they had been invited or not. They were a strange couple and people felt an empathy for them. People who had never met them, but had only heard stories about them, knew their names.

I was convinced (or at least I hoped) that I would meet Julia again. I didn't care about Ronald. She was extremely fit, apart from the injury to her ankle she had suffered when she slipped on the slope of the volcano. I knew that hadn't healed yet.

I decided to ask for further information from the nearest police station. Before I left the beach, I cast one last glance across the ocean.

"Bali," I said unconsciously. For the first time ever, I felt free of the exoticism of that word.

The mumbled roar of the ocean filed my head. I remembered Dionysus, the mythical Greek god Julia had talked about in her letter. He was the god of plant life and of wine, a symbol of fertile nature and of the ancient passion for life, companion of Apollo, who was worshiped as the youthful god of light (the sun). These two Greek gods played major roles in Friedrich Nietzsche's philosophy of art, which he expressed in *The Birth of Tragedy* and his essay "On Music and Words." Together these two works presented unrestrained emotion and intellectual clarity as forming a natural unity for the spontaneous formation of what was commonly considered to be culture.

The characteristics of the two gods were later expressed in a theatrical script I helped develop, which was tentatively called *The Way of Snow*. The play dealt with various themes: madness, poverty, and shamanism. It took place in three different worlds: the world of the Eskimo, Indonesia, and a large metropolis. It was a trilogy. A masked dance, it was like a silent movie, telling a story without using any words. The masks and music supported the drama and essentially formed a new sort of cross-cultural theater.

I don't know how long I stood facing the ocean. I remembered everything I had experienced with Julia, and then with Julia and Ronald. On my way back to Jakarta I had promised that I would help round out *The Way of Snow*. "It couldn't possibly be . . ." I thought as I felt a hand on my shoulder. "Julia!"

I didn't see Ronald.

"He's run out of marijuana. It has been a bad few days for him."

Over the next two months, we finished the scenario. Julia's vision determined the nature of the cast, which included local actors, especially men and women from Bali.

Using the name of Layar (Screen), the company performed in several big cities in Indonesia. The play was then produced in Europe, using a new cast.

In future years the work became the foundation of a new cross-cultural style of theater.

The play matched the experience of the world that had been recorded in a letter written while Julia was in Bali. A hybrid mixture inspired by the gods of various continents.

A Story within a Story

I received your poems in the post today. There was no name of
the sender or return address on the envelope. So I could only
guess. Perhaps you sent them, perhaps an American friend,
judging by the stamps. I don't know where you are—in Europe
or back in Indonesia again. It has been several months since we
last met in Jakarta.

I remember everything—the moment we met at the old
Halim airport. You took me to my hotel, your eyes shining
as brightly as ever. You never change! Afterwards I behaved
badly toward you for the whole month I was in Jakarta. I was
obsessed by you. I felt a mixture of love, of course, lust, quite
often, anger, from time to time, and even cynicism. My heart
was overwhelmed by the knowledge that they had tortured you
for such a long time. I was amazed that you weren't resentful,

despite what they did to you. In fact you were more affable, without any bitterness—or did I simply misunderstand you?

My feelings were a mixture of lust and darkness. I was at the end of a cycle that had lasted many years, arising out of some terrible experiences. While I was in Jakarta, I realized that I was behaving badly toward you, quite unforgivably. I was deliberately and utterly self-indulgent. Your poetry was beautiful again, filled with its old majesty, providing a huge electrical charge to our relationship. Now that we haven't seen each other for a while, and I'm back in Australia, having finally sorted out the tangled threads of my life, I think that it would be wonderful if we could meet again, considering that we're both feeling much calmer. I promise that I wouldn't treat you so despicably if we did.

I was looking for a lover in Jakarta, a demon who could drive away the other, worse, demons inside me. The last few months before I left Canberra to come to Jakarta, I had been trying to free myself from a man I met a year ago. He is someone important. A twenty-two-karat-gold VIP, a drunk, and a playboy. I became his lover. Eventually our relationship was discovered. I had to tell Bob about it. The press took an interest in us. There were even threats to kill my lover—that happened a fair bit. He had to hire a bodyguard. So did I.

My home has been in turmoil for a long time. I've been through a lot. It probably sounds strange to you, but I really felt that I needed to find a different lover. You are not the lover that

I need. Anyway, you indicated before that you were no longer interested, even if you were still sensitive to my needs.

If we were to go to Bali, as you suggested, and I would have really liked that, I would have been putty in your hands. And a prisoner of my own feelings. I thought I'd explode from the mixture of all those emotions I've already mentioned. It gave me a nightmare just thinking about everything. So I decided that if I stayed in Jakarta, and didn't go to Bali with you as we had originally planned, I'd eventually meet a demon who was just right for me.

And that was what happened. A well-built man, high status, with a blue Mercedes, and no brains. As thick as a brick, to use a common Australian phrase. He was very attractive, in bed and out of it. His stupidity soothed my nerves. He had no trouble getting his gear off. I've never been as physically satisfied as I was with him.

The logical consequence was that I would soon forget all about him. Isn't that strange?

Suzan

Canberra, November 1976.

I wouldn't have opened the letter again if her former husband, Bob (not his real name), hadn't visited Jakarta several years later. He brought me news about Suzan, his ex-wife. Bob was rising quickly in his career in the Department of Foreign Affairs. He was a real Australian aristocrat. Like Suzan, he was a member of the top social strata, with "important" family names on both sides, and newly rich. Bob was traveling around Southeast Asia on a mission, which obviously he couldn't tell me about.

Suzan was still important to him when he talked about her. I had first known them as a couple almost fifteen years ago. He was studying Indonesian literature and culture in Jakarta on a scholarship. Suzan was working as a local staff member at their national embassy. Perhaps Bob suspected that I wrote to his wife, but I wasn't sure whether he knew that Suzan and I were in a relationship, as she suggested in her letter.

Bob told me that Suzan was starting to make her mark as a writer. Her first book was a biography of a senior statesman and it had been well received by the critics. I had heard that from other sources as well. Suzan had told me that too when she came to Jakarta a few years ago, after her divorce. She was seeking to refresh her memory about her experiences when they lived in Jakarta. Suzan never mentioned her second book and I never asked her about it.

From what Bob said, it seemed that the second book had just been published. It was set in Jakarta.

"You play an important role in the book," he said. "Under another name, of course."

"Has the book been well received?"

"Not as well as her first book. The second book is a reasonably interesting spy story, spiced up with some details about social unrest in Jakarta during late 1965, when we were here."

"I presume you're in the book as well?"

"The major characters are all based on people we know. But it isn't entirely based on historical events and real people. Suzan invented some events and imagined the characters in the various situations. You appear in some very intimate scenes."

"I'm sorry I haven't read it. Suzan didn't tell me about it when she was here. But she didn't talk about her first book either. I hope she can use her experiences to grow as a writer."

"So do I. I hope she can find out who she is, now that she is a liberated woman."

"What about us men, Bob? How can we escape the limited fantasies and images that belong to old relationships, especially when they're over and gone?"

"Do you really mean that?"

"I do, Bob, I really do. The fantasies and images that appear in her novel are fiction, not fact, but they are woven around you, me, and Suzan. Does that make sense?"

"I'd like to be able to agree with you. But people don't just live in books. People in Canberra know me. They know Suzan too. Even you are part of my social circle there. As far as she is concerned, I suspect that you are 'the great absence.'"

"Perhaps, perhaps. But the Suzan we both know now is an innocent figure from the past. She has no need to change and no connection with past relationships. That's the impression I get from listening to you. I hope she will learn to write books that deal more constructively with events and people she has known."

"Maybe she will, maybe she won't. I'm not writer like you two. I still love her, even though we've been divorced for several years, even though it seems there's no way we can get back together again, especially after her second book."

"Perhaps that is one of the functions of literature, both for the author and the reader. Writing provides a way of closing off the past and opening new possibilities for future growth and development. This is not just a matter for the divorce courts."

"Do you love her?"

"Not any more. If we met again, we could be good friends but we would never be more than that. There is no way to bridge the gap between us."

After our conversation, I felt that Bob had found the answer to what he wanted to know. At least part of it. I opened Suzan's letter and read it several times. I wished I was a psychologist and could understand the deeper significance of each word and sentence in her long letter. It was a mixture of truth and fantasy, as though she was practicing to write her next novel, which would have nothing to do with me.

KASIM

Kasim was an ordinary man. So he was happy like everyone else and full of fervor when Indonesian independence was proclaimed on August 17, 1945, five years ago. And he really did feel liberated. Firstly, from the Japanese. From Takenchi, who used to slap him. Secondly, from the Dutch, who had returned with the British Army. He had served the Dutch as well. And thirdly, from his wife, especially after he joined the ranks of his village patrol, who were armed with bamboo spears. Before then, his wife regarded him (he thought) as useless. If he didn't exist, scores of other men could replace him as a clerk in the Statistics Bureau. That was how she seemed to feel, especially after the Japanese came and he couldn't adapt to the way in which circumstances had changed. "Adapt" meaning to work on the black market. Times had changed and in this new era the way to live was to become an operator on the black market, and being a black-market operator meant that one could live. Kasim didn't have the talent to operate on the black market. He did sell his wife's jewelry and some other things. But she stayed faithful to him. Her loyalty had given him the courage to survive the Japanese occupation of Indonesia, even if his guts were always tied in a knot.

But with the proclamation of independence his guts were restored to their normal condition, even though nothing in his life really changed. In fact, his life was more difficult than before, especially when fighting erupted throughout the whole city. If there was an exchange of gunfire in the alley between the local youths and the British soldiers, his eyes shone and his blood pounded vigorously as he stood on guard behind the closed door that led into his home. "If the Gurkhas dare attack us," he would tell his wife, "I will kill them all!" And looking at his wife as she sat calmly on the wooden sleeping platform, he vigorously waved his machete in the air.

He never had to defend his wife against the Gurkhas.

That was how he passed the first stage of the revolution.[1] Then the negotiations began. He didn't really understand what the arguments were about or why they couldn't be resolved, but he was loyal to the Republic. And his wife was loyal to him. But independence hadn't yet done anything to change their fate. His

1. The age of preparation, *zaman persiapan*, late 1945. The revolution lasted from 1945 to the end of 1949.

wife complained again. "It doesn't matter," he told her when she scowled, "the Republic will . . ." He never finished the sentence because, to be honest, he didn't know what the Republic would do. But eventually everything would work itself out.

Linggarjati came.[2] He was happy, then disappointed. Renville came.[3] He was happy and disappointed. His wife didn't change. She hoped for nothing and she was never disappointed. Meaning she never revealed her true feelings. She was faithful. And they lived. They did. Even though their neighbors and friends were amazed that they could live without an income. (Kasim refused to cooperate with the Dutch government. He was a "non-cooperator".) People wondered about Kasim and his wife. Or discussed them openly. Just as Kasim himself often wondered. How did his other non-cooperator friends live—people like Sakhand from the General Post Office, and Mihardja from the General Hospital? They were all amazed. And they all continued to live. And they all waited. And they were all loyal.

It never came to his attention that some people were saying that he could only survive as a non-cooperator because the Republican era provided many new opportunities for corruption. Others thought he was able to live because he was a clever black marketeer.

2. The Linggarjati Agreement was reached on November 15, 1945, between the Netherlands and the Republic of Indonesia. It recognized the Republic's de facto authority over Java, Madura, and Sumatra.
3. The Renville Agreement of January 17, 1946, was sponsored by the United Nations and attempted to remedy the failure of the Linggajati Agreement.

And had he heard them, Kasim would not have bothered to defend himself because everyone knew that he was a clerk in the Bureau of Statistics. What could he steal? At most, a few pens and pencils, some typing paper. It was true that in the early days of the Republic he had often stolen these items. Some he sold, some he gave to his children. At the time he didn't feel guilty or think that he might have done something that was even slightly immoral. His salary was simply too low. The paper was no longer officially useful now that the capital of the Republic had moved from Jakarta to Yogyakarta. So it was really waste paper. The proceeds of the paper he had sold before the Republic moved its capital to Yogyakarta were used to buy antiseptic to rub on his newly born son's navel. And to buy condensed milk to stimulate his wife's breasts.

But some people still thought he was a black market operator. Each morning he left his house clutching a briefcase. He only came home late in the afternoon. No one knew what he did all day. Even Kasim didn't know. He had a fixed routine. Precisely at eight o'clock each morning (according to his neighbour's Junghan clock), he left home to go to Senen. Kasim looked around the bookshops on the way. He never read any of the books. He certainly never bought any. At most, he flicked through the pages of the books and magazines. Feeling somewhat guilty, he particularly lingered over *Screen Romances*. Eventually he decided that his wife looked just like Ingrid Bergman. Ingrid, who symbolized a patient wife and mother, filled with understanding. Rita Hayworth's tantalizing smile made him feel rather embarrassed. He studied her photographs out of the corner of his eye and, if anyone approached him, he quickly turned to another page and pretended to be indifferent to the star. This was his one amusement.

The second part of his routine involved meeting other non-cooperators by the side of the road in Pasar Senin. "Did you hear Bung Hatta's speech last night?" one of them would ask. Or Bung Karno's speech. Or Pak Dirman's. At such moments, they no longer felt the sting of the sun, which was strong enough to melt the asphalt. "Merdeka!" they said when they met and when they left. Liberty!

The third part of his routine had him sitting in Fromberg Park. There were no prostitutes here during the day. So it was all right for a virtuous man like Kasim to be in the park.

When the meetings at Kaliurang went on endlessly and the Dutch and Indonesian leaders continually flew back and forth between Jakarta and Yogyakarta, he held no great hopes about the outcomes. But he didn't give way to despair. Deep down inside himself, Kasim was positive that everything would work out for the best eventually. He just didn't know when. But he was convinced. Absolutely convinced. Don't ask stupid questions. Fool. Kasim didn't feel that he was acting meritoriously. But when an announcement came from Yogya that the non-cooperators' valiant struggle was worthy of great respect, he smiled, and pointed rudely at Sutejo's house across the alley. Sutejo worked for NICA, the

Netherlands Indies Civil Administration. He had gone over to the enemy. Sutejo had joined the enemy.

The Second Military Action came.[4] Kasim was not disturbed. In his heart, he followed the Indonesian Army to the hills. To fight a guerrilla warfare. To attack. To ambush convoys. He killed at least twenty Dutch soldiers with his machete. In his imagination. He knew in advance about every attack on a Dutch convoy, before they were reported in the newspapers. But he said nothing. He was afraid that the NEFIS[5] might find out about him. It was enough that he himself knew. At most, he could talk to Sakhmud and Miharja. Because they were all non-cooperators.

Four years had passed. Kasim was still Kasim. Except that his wife didn't want to sleep with him. She didn't want any more children.

Finally the Round Table Conference was held.[6] He didn't feel happy about the accord that was achieved. It wasn't what he had hoped for. For the past few months, he hadn't spoken much with his wife. Every discussion seemed to end in a fight. So he had learned to be patient instead. To make concessions when necessary.

---

4. This Dutch military offensive against the Republic was launched in December 1948. The attack was successful but aroused strong international condemnation of the Netherlands.

5. The Netherlands East Indies Intelligence Service.

6. The Round Table Conference was held at the Hague from August 22 to November 2, 1949. It ended with the Netherlands agreeing to transfer full sovereignty to Indonesia.

To accept defeat as a step toward achieving his final goal. His final goal was to maintain peace with the woman who looked exactly like Ingrid Bergman. He had become a philosopher and often said, "Every difficulty is really an opportunity for a man of character." And wasn't little Kasim a man of character? So he gradually believed that he was a man of great character, the equal of the leaders who had taught him to be a man of character. And when Bung Karno came to Jakarta to give his end-of-year speech from the veranda of Gambir Palace, Kasim was not impressed, unlike the masses who stood crowded together to hear him. Some of them even cried. Not Kasim. Wasn't that him standing on the veranda, speaking to many thousands of citizens, including his own wife?

Yes, his wife, his wife, especially his wife. She must listen to his speech, the speech he had been thinking about and rehearsing for a long time. She must know that Kasim, her husband, was not just an ordinary man. He was a great man, just like Bung Karno. Would she understand what he was saying? Kasim was a national hero!

After the address, Kasim went home and slept. Tomorrow he would go to the main bus station. He would ask for a bus timetable to Yogyakarta. He wanted to study the schedules and find out the ticket prices. He would take a number 11 bus to the station. Board in front of the Catholic school in Menteng. The closest bus stop to his part of town, in Kalipasir.

The next day he asked his wife for some money. Without saying a word, she handed him the coins. Kasim left.

When he stopped the bus, the driver asked him, in Dutch, "Abonemen?" Are you a regular passenger? And before he could reply, the bus drove away. "NICA . . ." he cursed, but the bus quickly disappeared into the distance. An hour later he managed to take a bus to Lion Field and from there he walked to the Bureau of Statistics at Schoolweg South for the first time in a very long while. As he paced up and down in front of the office, he was suddenly greeted by a colleague and very old friend. Kasim was startled. He didn't like meeting people, especially someone who had gone over to the other side.

"Are you coming back to work?" the friend asked.

Kasim felt both embarrassed and angry. For some reason he did not understand, he replied, "No. I don't want to join NICA. I'm waiting for instructions from someone very senior . . ." He left immediately.

And Kasim was waiting for instructions. There were various possibilities as far as he was concerned. They all made him feel very happy. He would have liked to discuss them with his wife. But he didn't dare. So he kept them to himself. "Just wait," he told himself. "Once I receive my first salary, she'll change her attitude."

And Kasim waited. A month passed. His instructions had not yet come. Kasim no longer left his house. The instructions could come any time. But they never did. Finally he went to the Indonesian Delegation office to ask for an explanation. They asked him to leave his name and told him that he would have to wait.

Kasim waited. He wouldn't have minded the delay, except for the expression on his wife's face. Every day he played with his youngest child. He trained the parrot to call out "Tabek, Tuan!" Greetings, Sir! There was a reason for this training. When he received his first salary payment, he would hold a big feast and place the parrot at the front door. The bird would greet each guest on arrival. Especially those who had gone over to the Dutch. Members of NICA.

But the instructions didn't come. And so he was unsure about when the feast would be held. Kasim waited.

In February 1950, the time came to open parliament. And Kasim decided that he would finally leave the house. He had waited all morning. The post usually came late in the afternoon. Although it was forbidden to enter the grounds around Parliament from Sipayar Road, that was not a problem. There were loudspeakers at regular intervals in Lion Field, ready to broadcast President Sukarno's speech. He didn't know what the president would say. Bung Karno spoke clearly but Kasim's gaze was firmly fixed on the soldiers guarding him. Bung Karno said that Westerling[7] might attack at any time. Kasim wasn't afraid. But nothing happened and Bung Karno continued with his speech.

Kasim's attention was fixed on Lion Field. His mind was at rest and he remembered his childhood, going to school, playing

7. Raymond "Turk" Westerling (1919–87) was a Dutch military officer. He was denounced for war crimes but the matter was not pursued in the courts because of the stipulations of the 1949 transfer of sovereignty.

football, and the tall memorial in the middle of the stadium. Although he had fallen into a deep reverie, he was woken by the word "salary." He concentrated. His mouth hung open like the wide-open jaw of a thirsty man gulping in small drops of water. At first he heard some numbers describing how many civil servants there were in the Republican government service, or maybe they were those of the former Federal Civil Administration. (He wasn't sure which one and it didn't matter.) Bung Karno spoke of "the need to economize" and Kasim's heart began to pound. "Thank God, he's not talking about me," he thought. He heard the word "rationalization." This wasn't about him either. He listened more attentively to the loud voices projected across the field.

He heard the common abreviations for the salary regulations for Republican employees (the words drew him closer to the loudspeakers), then he heard the words "social justice" and "niveau" which he didn't understand at all. Then there were lots of calculations and numbers followed by lots of zeros. It was not his business and he waited. He was surprised at the way Bung Karno handled the figures. He himself hadn't done anything with figures for a few years.

But the speech continued and Kasim listened. When the loudspeaker said that it would be impossible to improve wages, Kasim agreed. He would be quite happy to be paid at his old salary. Then the loudspeakers compared the salaries paid to Dutch and Indonesian civil servants. (Kasim didn't agree but he repeated that he would be pleased to be paid his former amount.) The loudspeakers suggested that the difference shouldn't disturb people. It was rather unpleasant (an understatement, according to grammarians) as far as our own civil servants were concerned, but there were many other equally unpleasant things that civil servants and the masses would have to suffer in times to come. (I've suffered enough already, Kasim thought.) The situation is unavoidable. Our struggle is not yet over, and every struggle demands sacrifices. (I'm the one being sacrificed, thought Kasim.) Allow me once again to express our greatest possible gratitude to those civil servants classified as "non-cooperators," who have already suffered for many years and are currently leading lives of great difficulty, (Kasim accidently knocked his head against one of the coconut palms supporting a loudspeaker.) The glory of your names will live forever more. (Kasim sniffed his shirt. He had worn it constantly for the last two weeks.) The loudspeaker paused for a few minutes and then another voice said firmly, "Honorable members!"

'Have you finished?' Kasim wondered. Finished with non-cooperators. Finished with Kasim. The loudspeaker asked what other ways were available to reduce our debts. We're finished all right, thought Kasim. And he wondered about crossing Lion Field and going home.

Kasim mumbled as he repeated the words he had just heard. Your name will be honored forever more. Kasim is a man of great character. Kasim is a great man. Westerling is a great man.

Without his realizing it, he had arrived back at Kalipasar and was standing in front of his house, opposite Sutejo's house. Sutejo emerged and greeted him. "Liberty, comrade!"

Life around Lake Toba

I

When I first saw the large lake hidden in the folds of the pine-covered valleys, I was still seven kilometers away, at the top of a three-hundred-meter descent. The whole of Lake Toba is surrounded by steep cliffs, and the grassy plains at the top of the mountains provide extensive views in all directions. The island of Samosir lay in the middle of the lake like a sleeping giant tortoise. The whole world seemed to be asleep. The mountains formed blue layers, emphasizing the distance between themselves and the vast spaces that these distances contain. The lake is made of blue glass; had you thrown a rock, it would have shattered. Everything was close to everything else, forming a perfect unity. Strange small black dots moved across the glass lake. The ships were like flies trapped on a smooth surface. They slid slowly toward the villages in the valleys below, just as the buses crawled down along the winding roads past the sugarcane bushes and the rocks.

It was a market day. About fifty buses had come and fifteen ferries from different points on the lake. The boats brought fruit, vegetables, and handcrafts to be exchanged for the cargo carried by the buses. The buses came from Siantar and brought factory-processed goods like soap, matches, cigarettes, sugar, and kerosene.

Haranggaol is a place where people barter, where the economic ways of the city and isolated farming communities brush up against each other. The market is over in less than an hour. The buses climb back up to Siantar, more loaded than when they came. The ferries sail back to the villages at the edge of the lake and to Samosir, lighter than before but livelier and more colorful because of the gossip and city goods they carry.

After the terrifyingly steep drive along a narrow, unfenced dirt road, the bus in which I was traveling from Medan reached the market. The market was held on the beach and was crowded. There were lots of people and lots of boats, big and small. The market felt the same but it seemed different too. Many things had changed over the past five years. Ten years before then, during the Japanese occupation, and before that again, during European colonialism, there had only been the same five boats. "Now there are more than ninety," the mechanic told me. "There's less and less money to be made by selling tickets. The owners worship the passengers these days."

The vegetables were still the same: onions, beans, cabbages, some potatoes, bananas. However, large quantities of rice now came from outside. The valleys along the edge of the lake were fertile and well supplied with water, but the Island of Samosir was bare and barren. More than 120,000 people lived in the region. Recently, to use a contemporary term, the region was classified as "underdeveloped, with no possibility of change," despite the experimental use of machines to mill rice and to try to pump water from the lake onto Samosir.

The Highland Province of North Sumatra is isolated from passing traffic of all kinds. The east coast is rich. The Straits of Malacca are one of the major arteries for world trade.

But life goes on regardless. It wasn't quick, because it was faithful to every aspect of its past. Social institutions, folk arts, all those sort of things. Of course some things had changed.

Ninety ships on the lake clearly indicated that new ways were disturbing the old social limitations. There were newspapers and tinned goods. Schools flourished "like mushrooms in the wet season." There was a different mood in the air and this required negotiation with higher levels of government. The tranquility of the lake was an illusion that only tourists could entertain. The restlessness of modern life had entered the framework of isolated village life. Politics, price control, general elections, transmigration. But it was still undeniable that the basic rhythm of every movement and action continued to be inspired by old convictions, even if they now wore different faces.

I took a ferry across the lake to the valley where I had been born, Harian Boho, at the foot of Pusuk Buhit, opposite the Island of Samosir, which is a dead volcano peak in the center of an enormous crater. The owner of the boat approached me with a smile and said respectfully, "Your Excellency"—my father was an aristocrat in times gone by—"shames our customs. Please take your money back."

He did not want to accept money from me, and he insisted on taking me to the inlet where I was born, even though it was not part of his regular route. But had I refused, he would have felt humiliated.

A ferry like that could carry about 250 passengers on the upper deck and 250 on the lower deck. But if there were a lot more passengers, people could be jammed onto the canvas roof, which was meant to carry light items like baskets and woven fish traps. If there weren't very many people, they often gambled on the top deck, unless it rained, of course.

Some of the passengers sold coffee or ran food stalls. The whole trip could take from four to six hours, and the winds from the lake were often very cold.

On the lower deck, people sat facing each other. Those on the upper deck sat facing forward, as if they were at the movies. There was a high likelihood of meeting with friends or even kinsfolk. Everyone knew everyone else.

As soon as I boarded the boat, someone tapped me on the shoulder. I recognized him immediately. He was a friend, the same age as myself, someone I had played with when I was a child, from the "same mudhole" as people who kept cattle used to say.

After our asking about each other's family, and frequently commenting "Horas!" (Yes!), he told me more about himself. Besides his farming, he also caught fish. He showed me a fish trap made from sugar palm needles. He bought twenty traps at a time. Large traps. Twelve and a half rupiah each. A meter long, half a meter wide. Why so many? He kept half of them for himself and sold the rest to cover his costs in going to the market.

Our conversation shifted to rice growing. It was almost time to start hoeing the fields, now that the seeds were ready to sprout.

Someone asked what was the best kind of seed to plant this year. My age-mate, who was clearly regarded as an expert, gave a long and complicated reply. He knew which kind produced the most grain, this kind and that, and how much they all cost . . . Someone else asked him about the most auspicious day to plant the seedlings. My friend took out a notebook from his pajama shirt pocket and repositioned a supplementary sarung across his shoulders. Next Friday, the thirteenth of November. Why the thirteenth of November? It had to be an uneven number, in the first half of the month.

Astrology with a contemporary calendar. But everyone believed him. And of course he was right. I said nothing and he offered me a cigarette. I realized that I had not offered him one of my more expensive cigarettes. I was happy that my age-mate had accepted my sudden arrival, after such a long time, as perfectly normal.

The conversation moved to another topic. I listened as much as I could and avoided answering their questions as often as I could. It was more pleasant listening to them.

"How is Mr. Si Harotas?" The speaker took out some betel nut from a bag by his side.

"He's rich. Now he lives in Bamban, East Sumatra. He's left the village."

"Rich?"

"Filthy rich. He built his own house in the out-country. He has five hectares of fields. He has redeemed his house here as well."

"That's what happens when fortune is on your side. Before he had to sell everything he owned, even his wife's clothing. They were almost divorced because of his gambling habits."

I asked my age-mate about different things, confident he would know what was happening in the village. Two thousand rupiah for a water buffalo. If he was a very good working animal, perhaps five hundred more. The price of a hoe, twenty-five rupiah. Crocodile brand hoes were the best.

I learned from him that the district now had a doctor after the government's refusal for many years to provide any at all. One doctor for 120,000 people. And three small polyclinics, several hours' distance by motorboat.

He told me that there were three primary schools in our valley. Two went as far as third grade, the other to the sixth grade. There was a shortage of teachers. Four teachers had completed training at high school level. The others were graduates of their own schools.

I continued to say nothing. It was as if I were preparing my body to follow his different pace of life. The calmness of the lake and the peacefulness of the view helped. But it also made me feel distant from those who were sitting around me, breathing and thinking in their own way.

My age-mate offered me a banana. It was sweet and very fresh.

I had brought some books with me to read in the boat. They remained in my bag. I didn't need them

The sound of the boat's engine merged into the surrounding rhythms. The laughter of the gamblers on the top deck vanished from the mind of the mechanic as he studied the labels on my suitcases showing the distant places I had traveled.

II

On Mondays and Thursdays crowds of people come to the market that serves the western shore of Lake Toba and the west coast of Samosir. The isolated valley, which is normally lifeless, is visited by hundreds of small boats and two ferries. The market provides an opportunity to exchange city goods for agricultural and forest products. There are endless valleys behind the coastal ranges, with broad plains and thick forests hundreds of square kilometers long, extending as far as the west coast of North Sumatra and the Indian Ocean. People in the hills can earn extra money selling milled timber and making tiny canoes called *solu*.

Fishermen gather the night before the market in the bays, catching fish to sell the next day. Iskandar the barber, the man who makes fish traps, and the storyteller, who is on his way home from Medan, will possibly be there too. Market days are not just about trade. They are times to relax and enjoy oneself.

Once, traveling theater troupes came around after the harvest, bringing their own tents. There was no time to joke and be happy before then. The beating of drums would anger the gods.

There are no more theater troupes today. The actors are no longer available. They have been rounded up and trained to perform in the city and to welcome visiting foreign dignitaries.

Only gambling remains. Dice roll under the banyan tree, close enough to the market but far away enough not to be obvious, particularly if the police come from their post some three hours away.

If the police do come, the gamblers simply find somewhere else farther away or hide behind the walls of a nearby *kampung*.

Champion gamblers are highly revered, or at least treated with care. They are looked up to. Usually they are masters of classical fighting styles, dressed in traditional costumes including turbans made of black Chinese silk, coral bracelets, and rings with large colored stones. Around their necks they wear necklaces made of flints and jungle boar tusks.

Champion gamblers usually have a somewhat cunning look and are far more self-confident than most people because of their superior abilities. Or at least they used to be. These days champion gamblers dress in ordinary clothes and know little or nothing about the martial arts. Once gambling was an activity that required the invocation of divine spirits. It was an art form. Now it is just a business, like buying and selling lottery tickets at a night market. True gamblers today are village headmen, creative artists, romantics who wager everything for love, restless individuals who don't fit onto village society.

The old-style champion gamblers have disappeared, as have traditional political leaders, the heads of districts. The champion gamblers I knew when I was a child have now become diligent farmers cultivating cabbages. District chiefs have been replaced by councils of political leaders whose followers belong to parties that are as tightly defined as clans once were.

The young men who have gone abroad to seek their fortunes stay there, seldom returning home to celebrate the New Year. Some never return at all. Many emigrate to East Sumatra following friends or relatives who have gone there before them. They are not always aware that they will have to labor on commercial plantations.

They don't understand what they have heard about the presence of malaria in the nearby coastal swamps. Those who do return home sick with malaria, or having lost their wife or child, soon hear about other plantations and set out again, full of hopes.

Old Aman Doang is part of that vanished world too. He was a professional storyteller. He told stories at night to protect the sick and women who had just given birth. He was an outstanding singer and a clown as well. He had no wife at that time, which added to his uniqueness as far as the local inhabitants were concerned. He never owned his own house but camped wherever he landed. He was a very practical man.

On market days he used to broker the buying and selling of small boats. In previous times, it was the custom that the person selling a boat and the person who hoped to buy it would never talk directly to each other. They might sit face to face, but the bargaining was conducted through a broker. At a certain point, the buyer would slip an amount of money into the broker's hand. The broker would calculate how much money he had received and convey that figure to the seller. Bargaining proceeded through the broker and the precise price offered was only made known once a successful transaction had been concluded. A discussion with a new customer could begin if a first set of offers and counteroffers failed.

That was how Aman Doang lived in those days. His role has vanished from valley society now and bargaining for boats takes place openly and directly between the two parties.

"It costs ten rupiah to go from Medan to Siantar," he said, groping in his pocket and glancing sideways at me. He pulled out a ticket with the destination and cost of the trip written on it. The ticket was as big as a ticket to enter the movies. He crumpled it up and then hurled it out of the restaurant. We watched him throw the ticket away.

I sipped the thick black coffee in front of me and let the storyteller be master of the moment. He had just come back from the east, where he had taken his son on a ship to Java, to enrol at the Bogor Academy of Agriculture. He had also visited Belawan, where one of the members of his family worked as a foreman.

"Was the boat really made of iron?" someone asked. The storyteller looked at me to answer the question. "Of course it was," I replied. From the expression on the man's face, I couldn't tell whether he believed me. Then someone else asked, "Well, why doesn't it sink?"

"An iron pot doesn't sink if you put it on top of water carefully . . ." another person observed sagely.

"That's true . . ."

I tried to explain the secrets of water pressure, and how . . .

But the storyteller wanted to draw the attention of the group back to himself. He had a new tale. The vastness of the whole journey could be gauged by his listeners when he told them that the cost of the trip there and back was two hundred and fifty rupiah. It was more than people in this valley earned in a year for their backbreaking work.

"We almost left Butet's mother behind in Tebingtinggi," he said, referring to his wife. "The bus stopped there and she went to the market to buy betel. The dummy."

"When I was in Medan once," another man said, "I couldn't work out what all those people did for a job. It gave me a headache just looking at them. They were like a flock of goats . . ."

A few minutes later, when yet another new story had started, a rather dull fellow asked where Tebingtinggi was. No one laughed. The storyteller offered him an Aspro. The man was sick. He had a fever and was coughing a lot. He was wrapped up in a sarung and wore a fez. The fez was made of wool; it was tapered and had a tassel on top. To help him swallow the Aspro, the man borrowed the drink of the person sitting next to him.

Our storyteller left the coffee shop, his head filled with the unresolved thoughts common to many farmers, who begin each day's labors perched on a chair at a coffee shop.

He knew that once he had gone people would talk about him. He must be a happy man. He had taken his son to Java. Just like a district chief. He has plenty of land. Four working water buffalo.

"No," someone else pointed out. "He shares it all with four other men." Then followed an explanation of the advantages of forming a cooperative like that. "Imagine a man owns one water buffalo. If it gets sick and dies, he has nothing. But if he shares with other men, he owns part of each ox. And if a friend or family member comes to borrow something, you can tell him, 'Well, of course if it was up to me, I'd be happy for you to have it. But you'll need to talk to the others as well.'"

When the man with fever coughed, the conversation turned to sickness. The man was showing signs of tuberculosis, as far as the group was concerned. But what could he do in a situation like this? There was no medicine. The only doctor was a day's trip around the lake. Coughing blood was caused by an enemy casting spells.

The rice fields formed terraces along the sides of the valley, leading up to the steeper cliffs. Everywhere farmers had begun transplanting the young seedlings. The black mud mingled with the green of the plants. It was pleasant to behold. The barren cliffs had been shaped by volcanic lava deposited thousands of years ago. In turn, they led up to the plains above them, in the Barisan Mountains. The plains were covered with weeds and shrubs. They too were good to see at this time of day. Later in the day, the sun would burn the hillsides and the rocky cliffs, and the sense of peacefulness disappear.

Tens of walled villages were scattered throughout the rice fields, resigned to their poverty, just as the man with tuberculosis was resigned to his fate.

Church bells echoed through the lonely valley. It was not Sunday. The bells were calling the children to school, held in the churches. Only about ten percent of the children in the valley were enrolled in schools, and not all of them attended regularly, if at all. There were various reasons for this. The children had to help in the fields. The schools were too far away. The buildings were not big enough to hold all the pupils. Some parents and children were content with the pace of their isolated and closed society, and had no interest in becoming educated to participate in the wider, more dynamic world.

There was not even a bullock track in the valley. What was there to take in a cart? After the crops had been planted, the villagers might turn their attention to building a track to connect the valley with the road that ran around the edge of the lake. There were even plans to make a winding road to the top of the cliffs, through the pebbles, rocks, and clay.

The man with tuberculosis stood up, indicating that it was time for all of us to go. The others took their leave. I looked around the coffee shop. There were cupboards along the left wall. Behind the glass doors of the cupboards were bottles of cordial, empty distilled palm wine bottles, full bottles of beer, "marie biscuits," and a few cakes of soap.

There was an old sewing machine in one corner. Several pieces of brown drill cloth hung above the machine. The shop owner was also a tailor. And a farmer, with several rice fields.

He sat behind me, saying nothing. I thought of paying him but then I remembered my previous experience and just said that I was leaving. He replied respectfully, thanking me for my presence. The price of one cup of coffee wouldn't make him rich, he commented.

When I left the café, I looked at my reflection in the lake and decided that I needed a haircut. I went back inside and asked the owner where I could find a barber.

The owner knew a kinsman, Iskandar. All the people in the valley were related to each other. Iskandar only cut hair on market days. This was not a market day.

"I can call him for you this afternoon, if you'd like," the owner said. Who was Iskandar? I wondered.

Later that day, Iskandar sat me down in a folding wooden chair.

Iskandar (he had originally been baptized in church with the name of Alexander) cut my hair in the middle of the empty marketplace. He was another of my age-mates.

From time to time I could see evidence of Iskandar's skill in the mirror. I listened as he told me how he had changed his name. He stopped being a Christian and became a Muslim instead. The minister had refused to accept his son into the school. He had accepted other children in preference to Alexander's. So he changed his religion.

Then he told me that he had been excommunicated because he had participated in a pagan ceremony asking the Dewata Gunung Pusuk Buhit, the gods of Mount Pusuk, for their blessing. The minister disliked him owning so much land. Iskandar was now head of the local branch of the Muslim Masyumi Party. His enemy was head of the Christian Parkindo.

When he attended traditional feasts these days, he sat with some of his followers who had also become Muslims. They ate chicken, not pork.

Iskandar was now called *kalifah*, leader, although most people still referred to him as Alexander. They still invited him to eat pork. He coughed self-righteously and refused. Iskandar had begun to learn Muslim mystical chants and mantras.

SOURCE TEXTS

These translations are based upon *Ibu Pergi ke Surga: Kumpulan Lengkap Cerpen Sitor Situmorang* [Mother goes to heaven: The complete short stories of Sitor Situmorang], edited by J. J. Rizal (Depok: Komunitas Bambu, 2011).

The stories were originally published as follows:

GERBERAS
"Gerbera." *Mimbar Indonesia*, March 11, 1950, 9, 24.

AKBAR
"Akbar." *Siasat*, October 3, 1954, 23.

CHÉRI
"Chéri." *Siasat*, April 4, 1954, 25, 27.

S
"Kota S." *Siasat*, May 1954, 24.

MIDDAY MAIDEN
"Perawan Tengah Hari." *Siasat*, March 14, 1954, 24–25.

THIS ALWAYS HAPPENS WHEN IT RAINS
"Begitulah Selalu Kalau Hujan." *Konfrontasi*, July–August 1955, 45–47.

FIRST LOVE
"Ibu." *Tjerita*, February 1958, 7–8.

PRINCE
"Pangeran," *Siasat*, April 3, 1955, 23.

JAPANESE PROVERBS
"Gadis." *Tjerita*, January 1958, 6–8.

JATMIKA AND JAMIKO
"Jatmika dan Jatmiko." *Pangeran* (Bandung: Kiwari, 1963).

STORY OF A LETTER FROM LEGIAN
"Kisah Surat dari Legian." *Aktuil*, December 22, 1980, 56–59.

A Story Within a Story

"Suatu Fiksi dalam Fiksi." *Aktuil*, January 22, 1981, 74–75.

Kasim

"Kasim." *Danau Toba* (Jakarta: Pustaka Jaya, 1981), 26–37.

Life around Lake Toba

"Kehidupan Daerah Danau Toba." *Danau Toba*, 38–55.

ABOUT THE AUTHOR
AND THE TRANSLATOR

AUTHOR

SITOR SITUMORANG was born on October 2, 1924, in North Sumatra. The village of Harian Boho is located in a small, isolated valley on the west side of Lake Toba facing the island of Samosir. After spending his early years immersed in Batak culture, language, and religion, he was sent away at the age of seven to be educated in Dutch-medium schools in Balige, Sibolga, Tarutang, and Jakarta. His education came to an end when the Japanese invaded Indonesia in 1942. During the Japanese occupation he worked in local government offices, read widely in European literature, and entered journalism. His first marriage, in March 1944, produced four sons and three daughters.

After World War II, Sitor became widely known for his reporting on the Indonesian revolution against the Dutch, often from Yogyakarta, capital of the new Republic. He was imprisoned by the Dutch for several months in late 1948. Following the revolution, he lived in the Netherlands from 1950 to 1951 at the invitation of the Dutch government, and subsequently worked at the Indonesian Embassy in Paris from 1952 to 1953. Sitor began writing poetry in 1948 and is considered a member of Indonesia's literary modernist "Generation of 1945." Throughout his life he was a highly productive and very visible writer, publishing ten volumes of poetry and a number of larger anthologies, three volumes of short stories, and one collection of plays.

Sitor joined the Indonesian National Party in 1953 and became a vigorous spokesperson on the nature of national culture. He was a lecturer at the National Film Academy and studied film at the University of California (1956–57). At various times, Sitor represented the artistic community as a member of the National Assembly, the National Planning Assembly, the Emergency People's Consultative Council, and the Consultative Body for the Assessment of Higher Education. He was chairman of the pro-Sukarno Institute of National Culture from 1959 to 1965 and, following Suharto's accession to power, was imprisoned for seven years as a political dissident.

After regaining his freedom in 1976, he spent long periods abroad. He and his second wife, with whom he had one son, lived in The Hague (1982–90), Islamabad (1991–96), Paris (1995–99), and Jakarta (2001–5), before finally settling in the Netherlands once more. Despite living overseas, he remained actively involved in Indonesian cultural affairs, and as the son of a senior Batak chief regularly returned to Sumatra to fulfill various traditional ritual duties. He also wrote a number of books on Batak regional culture and history.

Sitor Situmorang died in the Netherlands on December 20, 2014, and was buried in Harian Boho on January 1, 2015.

Translator

HARRY AVELING holds the degrees of Doctor of Philosophy in Malay Studies from the National University of Singapore, and Doctor of Creative Arts in Creative Writing from the University of Technology, Sydney. He is an honorary full professor in the Department of Translation and Interpreting Studies, Monash University, Melbourne, Australia. His recent publications include translations of *Pilgrimage* by Isa Kamari (Ethos Books, 2016), *Kill the Radio* by Dorothea Rosa Herliany (3rd printing; MataAngin, 2017), and *Why the Sea is Full of Salt and Other Vietnamese Foktales* by Minh Tran Huy (Silkworm Books, 2017). He translated Sitor Situmorang's *Oceans of Longing* (Silkworm Books, 2018) with Keith Foulcher and Brian Russell Roberts. A collection of essays on translation and Indonesian/Malay literature is forthcoming from the National University of Malaysia Press.